LAUREL THE WOODFAIRY
by Cassie Kendall

Laurel isn't like most woodfairies. She's more energetic than elegant. More adventurous than artistic. And certainly more curious than quietly content. She's even interested in the Great Forest. But no woodfairy ever leaves the peaceful Dappled Woods.

Then for the first time in ages, a stranger arrives in the fairy woods. The visitor is a pixie named Foxglove. Laurel befriends him while daring to keep his presence a secret.

But Laurel fears she's made a mistake when Foxglove disappears. Especially when the fairies' most precious possession vanishes at the same time.

To track down both, Laurel sets out into the Great Forest. However, fearsome creatures lie in wait for her. And before long, Laurel finds herself face-to-face with a deadly enemy.

STARDUST CLASSICS SERIES

LAUREL

Laurel the Woodfairy

Laurel sets off into the gloomy Great Forest to track a new friend—who may have stolen the woodfairies' most precious possession.

Laurel and the Lost Treasure

In the dangerous Deeps, Laurel and her friends join a secretive dwarf in a hunt for treasure.

Laurel Rescues the Pixies

Laurel tries to save her pixie friends from a forest fire that could destroy their entire village.

ALISSA

Alissa, Princess of Arcadia

A strange old wizard helps Alissa solve a mysterious riddle and save her kingdom.

Alissa and the Castle Ghost

The princess hunts a ghost as she tries to right a long-ago injustice.

Alissa and the Dungeons of Grimrock

Alissa must free her wizard friend, Balin, when he's captured by an evil sorcerer.

KAT

Kat the Time Explorer

Stranded in Victorian England, Kat tries to locate the inventor who can restore her time machine and send her home.

Kat and the Emperor's Gift

In the court of Kublai Khan, Kat comes to the aid of a Mongolian princess who's facing a fearful future.

Kat and the Secrets of the Nile

At an archaeological dig in Egypt of 1892, Kat uncovers a plot to steal historical treasures—and blame an innocent man.

Design and Art Direction by Vernon Thornblad

This book may be purchased in bulk at discounted rates for sales promotions, premiums, fundraising, or educational purposes. For more information, write the Special Sales Department at the address below or call 1-888-809-0608.

Just Pretend, Inc.
Attn: Special Sales Department
One Sundial Avenue, Suite 201
Manchester, NH 03103

Visit us online at www.justpretend.com

LAUREL
the Woodfairy

by Cassie Kendall

Illustrations by Joel Spector
Cover Art by Patrick Faricy
Spot Illustrations by Kazuhiko Sano

Stardust
CLASSICS

Just Pretend, Inc.
Attn: Publishing Division
One Sundial Avenue, Suite 201
Manchester, NH 03103

Stardust Classics is a registered trademark
of Just Pretend, Inc.

Second Edition
Printed in Hong Kong
04 03 02 01 00 99   10 9 8 7 6 5 4 3

Publisher's Cataloging-in-Publication
(Provided by Quality Books, Inc.)

Kendall, Cassie.
Laurel the woodfairy / by Cassie Kendall; illustrations by Joel Spector; spot illustrations by Kazuhiko Sano. -- 2nd ed.
p. cm. -- (Stardust classics. Laurel; #1)
SUMMARY: Laurel is kidnapped by trolls while trying to recover the Crystal of the Chronicles, which is essential to the woodfairies' celebrations.
Preassigned LCCN: 97-73128
ISBN: 1-889514-05-5 (hardcover)
ISBN: 1-889514-06-3 (pbk.)

1. Fairy tales. I. Spector, Joel, 1949- II. Sano, Kazuhiko, 1952-
III. Title. IV. Series.

PZ8.K46La 1998   [Fic]
                                  QBI98-678

Contents

CHAPTER ONE

Laurel's Tune

t's no use!" cried Laurel. "I just can't play this tune!"

Laurel lowered her flute. Her beautiful fairy wings drooped as she thought about the long hours she'd spent practicing.

Today her lesson had started out so smoothly. At first her fingers had skipped merrily over the holes of the flute. But as the music went faster, the notes started piling up on top of each other. The next thing Laurel knew, her fingers were skidding and the flute was squeaking.

Now Laurel sadly looked up at her music teacher, Mistress Marigold.

"I give up," said Laurel. "I'll never be ready for the Celebration of the Chronicles. All the other woodfairies will have some wonderful poem or picture or dance to share. But I won't have a thing to contribute."

Mistress Marigold gently patted Laurel's arm. Of all Laurel's teachers—in fact, of all the fairy elders—she was the kindest.

"When it's time, your song will come out just right," Mistress Marigold said.

Laurel sighed. "I've never played it all the way through without making a mistake. Why can't I write an easy tune?"

Mistress Marigold was silent for a moment. "You haven't told me what your tune is about," she finally said. "What does it describe? The first snowfall of winter? The journey of a stream through the woods? A rainstorm on a hot summer night?"

Laurel thought. Then she said, "I don't know. It's just music."

"I'm sure it's about something," Mistress Marigold told her. "You just don't know what that something is yet. When you do know, you'll be able to play it perfectly. But it's late now, and you've had enough practice for today. Come and see me again tomorrow if you'd like another lesson."

Laurel put her flute into her bag and said good-bye. "Don't worry, Laurel," Mistress Marigold called after her. "Just keep thinking about what your tune says."

Laurel left her teacher's simple wooden cabin and headed back to her own treehouse.

"The Celebration's in just a few days," she said. "What am I going to do?"

This was the first year Laurel was old enough to take part in the ceremony. And she was sure she'd make a complete fool of herself. Worst of all, she was going to make Mistress Marigold look like a poor teacher.

Laurel walked a bit and then flew a bit—as she often did when worried. Of course, woodfairies don't fly so much as they glide. When you're nearly four and a half feet tall, you can't fly very high or very far.

Soon Laurel reached a fairy cabin that jutted out from a huge elm tree. On the porch stood Mistress Gooseberry, the art teacher. With her was Primrose, a young fairy about Laurel's age. Mistress Gooseberry was looking at a painting that

Primrose had just finished.

"Very good," said Mistress Gooseberry to Primrose. "This will make a fine contribution to the Celebration."

Mistress Gooseberry was frowning, and her arms were folded. It seemed to Laurel that Mistress Gooseberry always sounded cross—even when giving praise. Not that Laurel had ever gotten much praise from Mistress Gooseberry.

Just that morning during her art lesson, Laurel had failed again. She'd been trying to paint lightning jumping from cloud to cloud. But she'd put too much paint on her brush. She'd ended up with a big blob of yellow.

To make matters worse, Primrose had flown by just then. Of course, she'd had to say something about Laurel's mistake. And about how strange it was to draw something nasty like a thunderstorm. Primrose never made mistakes. *She* would do something perfect for her first Celebration.

Laurel turned away from the cabin. With her head down, she walked silently through the woods. For once she didn't notice the bright flowers and sparkling sunlight of the Dappled Woods. Nor did Laurel see her good friend Ivy until she bumped right into her.

"Ivy! I'm sorry!" exclaimed Laurel. "I wasn't looking where I was going. As usual."

"That's all right," Ivy told her. "I'm glad to see you. You're just in time to watch my dance. It's the one I'm practicing for the Celebration."

Though Ivy was shy and soft-spoken, she didn't mind performing in front of others.

"I'd love to see it," said Laurel.

Ivy moved to a space between the trees. She began her dance curled up in a ball on the ground. Ever so slowly and gracefully, she rose to her feet. Then she stretched her arms and fingers toward the sky. She trembled and swayed a bit, as if gently bobbing in the wind.

Laurel smiled. Ivy had perfectly captured how a violet blooms in the spring.

Laurel clapped her hands. "It was beautiful, Ivy! You don't need any more practice. Your dance will be a wonderful contribution to the Celebration."

"Thank you, Laurel," said Ivy. She fell into step beside her friend. As they walked, Ivy asked, "Are you going to do a dance too?"

Laurel chuckled a bit sadly. "I don't think so," she said. "Don't you remember my last dance lesson?"

Ivy smiled gently. "Oh yes. Now I do. You tried to swirl like autumn leaves caught in a winter wind. You kept spinning around and around until—" She paused and blushed.

"It's all right, Ivy. I'm the one who brought it up. Yes, I got my wings and legs tangled and fell down."

"It made me dizzy just watching you," said Ivy.

Both fairies broke into giggles.

"Leaves in a whirlwind!" Ivy laughed. "I don't think a fairy ever tried to do that kind of dance before. But then you're not like most fairies," she said.

"I guess I'm not," admitted Laurel.

"Well, I'm glad you're not," said Ivy. "Anyway, I'd be happy to help you practice."

Laurel was touched by Ivy's offer. "Thanks, but I'm going to play a tune on my flute."

Seeing Ivy's interest, Laurel quickly added, "Don't ask me what it's about. I don't know myself yet."

"I'm sure it will be lovely," Ivy said.

Ivy's words cheered Laurel. She even began to whistle the tune she planned to play.

But the whistle died on her lips as they entered the Ancient Clearing. This was where the Celebration would take place.

The Ancient Clearing was a beautiful glade in the heart of the woods. Long ago the fairies had carefully woven the branches of young trees together. Now the trees towered high overhead. Late afternoon sunlight sifted through the leaves. Laurel thought that the clearing looked like a huge room with grand, green-tinted windows.

To one side of the glade stood a polished tree stump. It had been carved out to create a cabinet-like space. Behind its doors rested the Crystal.

The Crystal was a large, lovely stone, shaped much like a diamond. Its rough edges had been smoothed and polished until they sparkled. But the most important thing about the Crystal was what it held. For the stone was hollow. And inside, the fairies placed their most valuable possession: the Chronicles. The Chronicles was a book that told the whole history of the woodfairies.

Now Laurel and Ivy paused in front of the stump. "It's almost time for the Celebration," said Ivy. "I'm excited! Especially since we get to take part this year."

Ivy thought for a moment before going on. "You know, lately I've spent all my time practicing my dance. I haven't even started to think about what to record."

That was another part of the ceremony. Each fairy was asked to add to the Chronicles a memory of the year gone by.

"Neither have I," said Laurel. "But maybe after the elders hear my flute, they won't even ask me."

Ivy laughed. "That would never happen. Besides, I know you'll do a wonderful job." Then she waved good-bye and walked off toward her house.

But Laurel remained in front of the stump, thinking. Her contribution to the Celebration had to be just right. It should capture the beauty and peace of the woods.

"Please let my tune do honor to the Celebration," Laurel whispered in a soft voice. She left the clearing and headed for her own home.

Laurel had chosen to build her house high in the branches of a huge oak. Most fairies liked to live near the ground. But Laurel loved being close to the breeze, birds, and sunbeams.

Though there was a ladder leading up to her treehouse, Laurel didn't often use it. Usually she flew straight to the top. Today she was too worried to fly. Instead, she slowly climbed up.

Laurel's heart lifted as she entered her cheerful home. The big room was alive with color. Shelves were carved into the walls. And each was filled with rocks, shells, or feathers that Laurel had found. On the wooden floor were pretty rugs the young fairy had woven. A filmy canopy covered her bed.

Laurel hung up her cloak and placed her bag on a shelf. Then she picked up her journal. Every day, every fairy wrote an account of what she had done. Just as the Chronicles told the history of all fairies, a fairy's journal told her own history.

Now Laurel thought about what she would write in her journal for today. "I'm not really sure I want to remember what happened," she said with a sigh.

Journal in hand, she walked to a window and brushed

aside the curtains. Below she could see Thunder Falls—the highest and loudest waterfall in the Dappled Woods. Fairies usually liked places that were peaceful and quiet. But not Laurel.

Laurel let the curtains fall back into place. "Maybe I'll take my journal down by the waterfall," she said softly.

She put her cloak back on and glided to the ground. After settling on a rock near the pond, she began to write.

A sudden movement at the edge of the pond caught Laurel's attention. A tiny head poked through the long grass. It was her friend Mistletoe the mouse.

Laurel got down off the rock and stretched out on the grass. She propped her chin on her hands so that she was face-to-face with Mistletoe. "Hello!" she said. "What have you been up to lately?"

Laurel had learned the forest animals' language. But she hadn't told many of the other woodfairies about that. She hadn't even written about it in her journal. Everybody thought that she was strange enough as it was. And talking to animals was not a common woodfairy activity.

Mistletoe wiggled her nose. "I went exploring all the way to the edge of the Dappled Woods. Where the Great Forest starts."

"How exciting!" said Laurel. Like all other fairies, Laurel had never been outside the Dappled Woods.

Mistletoe nervously scratched her ear. "I don't know," she said. "Something seemed wrong."

As Mistletoe spoke, Chitters the chipmunk joined them. Chitters was another of Laurel's animal friends. Now he twitched his furry tail and asked what was going on.

"Mistletoe is worried that something's wrong in the Great

Forest," Laurel reported.

Chitters flicked his ears. "Worry, worry. No point in it, I say."

"Mistletoe doesn't worry without a good reason," began Laurel. But she was interrupted by the mouse.

"Listen!" Mistletoe squeaked.

Laurel and Chitters fell silent. If sharp-eared Mistletoe gave a warning, it was best to pay attention.

Then they heard it. An unfamiliar noise in the bushes behind them.

Mistletoe sniffed the air wildly. "A stranger!" she exclaimed. "Hide!"

At once the two animals disappeared into the brush.

"A stranger?" Laurel questioned. "But—"

Before she could say another word, someone bumped hard against her. Whoever-it-was tumbled to the ground with a thud.

Laurel jumped to her feet. Someone had tripped over her!

Laurel saw that whoever-it-was had fallen flat on her face. She'd never heard of a fairy who tripped over other fairies before! Except maybe for herself.

Then Laurel noticed something very odd about the other fairy's back. She had no wings! This wasn't a fairy at all!

CHAPTER TWO

An Unexpected Guest

ho are you?" Laurel asked. "What are you? And what are you doing here?"

The creature scrambled to her feet. She brushed off a thick layer of dirt and moss.

"That doesn't sound very welcoming," said the creature.

Laurel took a closer look. This wasn't a "she"—it was a "he"! And there weren't any "he's" among the woodfairies.

"You're a…a…" Laurel stammered. She tried to remember what she'd heard about wingless creatures like this one. They lived deep in the Great Forest. The woodfairies hardly ever talked about them.

The stranger was a little shorter than Laurel. Though he was thin, he looked very strong. Shaggy black hair, the same color as his eyes, fell to the collar of his cloak. The cloak itself was the dull greenish brown color of winter leaves. Underneath it he wore a tunic made from old fish skins. The scales made a nice pattern, but it wasn't the cleanest outfit in the world. It even smelled a bit fishy. Who would wear such a thing?

Then the newcomer tossed his head impatiently. Sharply pointed ears peeked out from underneath his dark hair.

Suddenly Laurel remembered what this creature was called. "You're a pixie!" she cried.

"So I am!" exclaimed the stranger.

Laurel knew that the other woodfairies didn't approve of pixies in the least. So she was a bit scared.

Then Laurel saw her animal friends creep out from their hiding places. Knowing that they were still nearby made her feel braver.

The pixie gave a little bow. "Foxglove's my name," he announced. "And scavenging's my game."

"Scavenging?" asked Laurel in surprise.

"You know. The fine art of using the unused. Wanting the unwanted. Treasuring the untreasured. Just generally picking up things that others throw away. Surely you've heard of me. Some say I'm the most famous scavenger in the entire Great Forest," finished the pixie.

Laurel frowned. "I've never heard of *any* scavengers," she said coldly. "No fairy would ever be interested in something like that. Why, it sounds…dirty!"

At least Laurel was sure that most fairies would think so.

"Besides, you can't scavenge around here," Laurel went on. "Everything in the Dappled Woods stays in its proper place. Every acorn. Every leaf. Every twig."

Laurel was certainly exaggerating. But she wanted to get rid of this stranger. She knew what Mistress Gooseberry would say about talking to a pixie. Even Mistress Marigold might be shocked.

"Then I guess what everybody says about woodfairies is true," said Foxglove.

"Everybody who?" Laurel asked. "What does 'everybody' say?"

"That woodfairies are downright prissy."

"Prissy!" exclaimed Laurel. "Well! Everybody I know says

that pixies are rough and dirty!"

"Rough and dirty?" shot back Foxglove. "Hah! Let me tell you, rough and dirty is what real life is all about! But of course, you fairies wouldn't know that. You never leave the Dappled Woods!"

They were both speaking rather loudly now—almost shouting. Laurel saw that Chitters and Mistletoe were staring at her.

If there's one thing woodfairies dislike, it's shouting. And Laurel was no exception. So she tried to control her temper.

Anyway, she knew the stranger was right about one thing. Woodfairies never went outside the Dappled Woods.

"You still can't take anything," Laurel said, speaking more quietly. "The other fairies won't allow it."

Foxglove had calmed down by now too. He thought about Laurel's words. Then he grinned. "Perhaps we could agree to a trade."

Laurel began to sputter. "A trade? Don't you understand what I've been saying? I won't even trade you anything from our woods."

"Who cares?" said Foxglove. "There's nothing in your woods that could possibly interest me anyway. I'm in the market for something really special. Something different. Something rare."

Foxglove was warming up now. He waved his hands grandly as he spoke.

"A necklace with a pearl missing. A gold watch with a broken spring. A piece of chipped china. You wouldn't have anything like that around, would you?"

"And what if I did?" asked Laurel, growing curious. "What do you have that I could possibly want to trade for it?"

Foxglove reached into a pocket. "How about this?" he exclaimed.

"A pinecone?" asked Laurel. "But you took that from us!"

"Oh no," said Foxglove. "This pinecone isn't from the Dappled Woods. It's from a mysterious land far, far away. This is no ordinary pinecone, believe me."

"It looks like any other pinecone to me," said Laurel. "Why would I want it?"

Foxglove suddenly looked downhearted. "Do you mean," he said, "we don't have a trade?"

"Of course we don't," said Laurel. "I think you should just go home now. Before any of the other fairies see you."

Foxglove stared at her. Then, to Laurel's surprise, he sank down to the ground. He put his grubby face into his grubby hands and sobbed.

"I can't go home," he blubbered. "Not empty-handed. Not again. Not after I told everybody that I'd come back with something really special."

"I thought you were the most famous scavenger in the entire Great Forest," said Laurel.

"I lied," moaned Foxglove. "I'm a failure. I wouldn't be able to scavenge an acorn if it fell right on top of me."

Laurel knelt beside the pixie and patted his shoulder. She felt sorry for him, but she didn't know what to say. She'd never had to deal with a problem like this. How would the other fairies handle it?

She knew the answer to that question. The other fairies would get the pixie out of the Dappled Woods as soon as possible.

Almost as if he had read her thoughts, Foxglove looked up at her. "Can I stay here for a little while?" he asked. "Just until I figure out what to do? I've been traveling for days. It's late, and I'm tired. I could really use a good night's sleep."

Laurel was about to say no. But then she remembered Mistress Gooseberry's frowning face. And she realized she was looking at Foxglove in just the same way.

"All right," she said at last. "I guess you can stay here tonight. Somewhere."

"Oh, I don't need much space," Foxglove said. "Where do woodfairies live, anyhow?"

"I live up there," Laurel answered, pointing to her tree-house.

Foxglove looked up. He whistled. "I'd like something a little closer to the ground," he said. "Is there an empty rabbit hole I could hollow out?"

"You'd sleep in a hole in the ground?" Laurel asked.

"I *live* in a hole in the ground. Our whole pixie village used to be a rabbit warren."

"Don't tell me. You scavenged it," said Laurel.

"Yes, we did," said Foxglove proudly. "After the rabbits moved to New Warren, we took over the old one. Dug out the holes until they were pixie-sized."

"Well, maybe there's an old rabbit hole around here somewhere," said Laurel. She turned to her animal friends.

The pixie seemed to notice Chitters and Mistletoe for the first time. "Hey, what are they doing here?" he asked.

"They're my friends," said Laurel. She introduced them to Foxglove. Chitters trilled a long, noisy greeting. And Mistletoe gave a friendly hello. Foxglove just stared at them.

Then Laurel asked the animals, "Do you know of any holes big enough for him?"

Chitters didn't have any suggestions. But he loved having a new audience. The chipmunk started chattering. "He's too big to stay with me. Huge! Enormous! Much too big!"

Mistletoe broke in. "I have an idea," she said. Laurel turned to her thankfully. She could usually count on the clever little mouse.

As Mistletoe went on, Foxglove looked from the mouse to Laurel in surprise. "Are they talking to you?" he asked. "Nobody told me that fairies could talk to animals!"

"Well, most fairies can't," said Laurel.

"You're a bit unusual, aren't you?" laughed Foxglove.

Laurel chose to ignore that. Instead she asked, "Do you want Mistletoe to show you where you can stay?"

"Sure," said Foxglove.

Mistletoe led them around the pond to the other side of the waterfall. The mouse used her sharp teeth to pull aside a branch. Behind it was a deep space lined with moss and dried leaves.

"This will be fine," said the pixie. He crawled into the hollow and pulled the branch across the opening. "See you in the morning," he called.

Laurel stared at the branch for a moment. "Don't you want something to eat?" she asked. But the only answer she got was a soft snore. The pixie had already fallen asleep.

"Well, he certainly makes himself right at home," Laurel said.

With her animal friends alongside her, Laurel wandered back to the pond. She picked up her journal and dusted it off. Saying good-bye to Mistletoe and Chitters, Laurel headed up to her treehouse.

Later, as she sat on her porch, Laurel again thought about her journal. What should she write? Did she dare tell about meeting a pixie? What if one of the mistresses read her journal? Would she be angry that Laurel let a stranger stay in the Dappled Woods?

Then Laurel reminded herself that the pixie would leave tomorrow. None of the other fairies would even know he'd been there. And Foxglove didn't seem like the type to make any trouble.

At least that's what Laurel hoped.

CHAPTER THREE

A Misplaced Pixie

hen Laurel got out of bed the next morning, she went straight to her porch. Looking down, she saw no sign of Foxglove.

Was he still asleep? Or had he already left the Dappled Woods?

Laurel thought about fixing herself breakfast. But she decided she had to find out whether the pixie was really gone.

She hurried down to the waterfall. "Foxglove!" she called. "Are you there?"

No answer. Perhaps he was sleeping too soundly to hear. Laurel pushed the branch aside. The hollow was empty.

"So he's really gone," Laurel said to herself. "Well, it's all for the best. Now I won't have to worry about other wood-fairies finding out about him."

She leaned back and sighed. "But he could have at least said good-bye."

There was a noise at her feet. Laurel glanced down to see Mistletoe.

"Looking for somebody?" the mouse asked with a twitch of her whiskers.

"Just Foxglove," said Laurel.

"I know where he is," replied Mistletoe.

"He's still around?" Laurel asked. "Where?"

"Follow me," said Mistletoe. She led Laurel to a bush heavy with blackberries. Then she scampered off.

Foxglove was sitting on the ground, breakfasting on berries. His hands and lips were stained with juice.

"Hi, Laurel!" Foxglove called out with a happy wave. "Hope you don't mind my picking a few berries."

"No," replied Laurel. "After all, you have to eat something before you leave."

Foxglove reached for another berry. "Oh, I've decided to stay for a while," he announced.

"What? But you can't stay here," said Laurel.

"Why not?" asked Foxglove. He got up, licked his lips, and wiped his hands on a leaf. "I think I'll fit right in."

"Fit right in!" exclaimed Laurel. "With woodfairies? But you're a pixie."

"Not your usual pixie," objected Foxglove. "I'll be right at home here."

"I don't think so," said Laurel slowly.

"Come on, give me a chance," Foxglove begged. "Let me meet some of your friends. Before long, they'll forget I'm a pixie."

"No, they won't," Laurel said.

"Why not?" asked the pixie.

Laurel answered slowly. "Woodfairies have wings, for one thing."

"From what I've seen, wings are no big deal," said Foxglove. "You don't seem to do much flying."

Laurel tried again. "We don't live in holes in the ground."

19

"Do you all live in treetops?" Foxglove asked with a shiver.

"No," admitted Laurel.

"Well, then," said Foxglove. "Anywhere is fine. Just as long as it's on the ground. Like the hollow by the waterfall."

Laurel sighed. "All right," she said at last. "I'll show you how woodfairies live. You'll see for yourself that this isn't the place for you."

"Great!" Foxglove said. "And I can meet some other fairies, right?"

"Not unless you want to leave a lot sooner than you'd planned. I'll let you look around. But you've got to promise to stay out of sight."

"Okay," agreed Foxglove.

So they set out. Laurel headed toward the Ancient Clearing. She knew that they would find more fairies there.

Just outside the clearing, Laurel stopped Foxglove. Carefully they hid behind a bush and peered through the leaves.

"There they are," Laurel whispered.

Foxglove stared in curiosity. Several fairies were planting seeds around the edges of the clearing. One was weaving reeds into a basket. Another was gathering fallen pinecones.

"What are they doing?" asked Foxglove.

"What woodfairies do," explained Laurel. "Taking care of the forest and helping things grow. Making things. And keeping the woods neat and clean."

Foxglove looked at Laurel. "They sure dress differently than you do," he said. He turned back and studied the simple clothing the other fairies were wearing.

"I know," sighed Laurel. She looked down at the swirling

pattern of her own dress. "I'm different in lots of ways."

Foxglove shrugged. Then he pointed to a young fairy. She was opening up the tree-stump cabinet where the Crystal was kept.

"What's she doing?" the pixie asked. His eyes grew large as he caught sight of the beautiful stone in the fairy's hands. "And what's that? It's wonderful!"

"That's the Crystal of the Chronicles," Laurel told him. "And she's going to polish it for the Celebration."

"Celebration?"

Laurel explained. But by the time she'd finished, Foxglove looked half asleep.

"Let me get this straight," he said. "You hold this Celebration to honor your Chronicles. And the Chronicles tell about woodfairy history. But your history never changes. You do the same thing year round, every year. You dance, paint, and sing."

"That's right," said Laurel. "The first words of every year's entry are the same. It always begins with 'We did many beautiful, creative things this year.'"

"I don't want to sound rude," said Foxglove, scratching his head. "But that sounds kind of—well—boring."

Laurel was stunned. She'd never heard anybody say such a thing before.

"It's not boring!" she exclaimed.

But even as she said it, she found herself wondering whether Foxglove had a point. Was something missing from woodfairy life? Some variety, perhaps? A little adventure?

After a while, Foxglove sat back. "I see younger fairies. And some that look older."

"Yes, the older ones are called elders," said Laurel. "You're a student until you decide what you want to do. Then, once the older fairies think you're ready, they invite you to be an elder."

"What do elders do?" asked Foxglove.

"They practice their art or craft. Some—they're called 'mistresses'—teach."

Foxglove nodded slowly. "So there are young fairies. And elders. But I don't see any babies. Where are they?"

"There are no babies," Laurel explained. "A woodfairy springs from the head of a dandelion when it's touched by the light of the full moon. We grow to almost our full size in a matter of moments."

"No babies," Foxglove said softly. "I'd miss babies."

Laurel and Foxglove watched a bit longer. Then they made their way back to the pond by Laurel's treehouse.

When they got there, Foxglove sat down on a rock. Laurel sat beside him. Both were quiet for a few moments.

"Maybe you're right," said Foxglove at last. "Maybe I don't belong here. But I still can't go home. Not without something to take back."

"What will you do?" Laurel asked in a worried voice.

"I don't know," said Foxglove with a sigh. "I wish I could talk to the animals like you do. Then I could just live in the woods, with animals for company."

"But that sounds so lonely," said Laurel. She had to think of some way to help Foxglove.

Then she had an idea. "You only have trouble with your scavenging, right?" she asked. "Otherwise, you can do pretty much everything that other pixies do, can't you?"

"Pretty much," said Foxglove. "But scavenging is so important."

"Then I'll help you," said Laurel. "If we work together, I know we can find something for you to scavenge."

Foxglove looked doubtful. "Something special? And different? And rare?"

"Yes," replied Laurel. Then she paused. "But I don't think we'll find anything here in the Dappled Woods. At least not anything that I could let you take. No, we'll have to look somewhere else."

"But fairies never leave the Dappled Woods," objected Foxglove.

"It's about time we did, don't you think?" said Laurel. Indeed, the idea of being the first fairy to explore the Great Forest appealed to her.

"You wouldn't like it out there," answered Foxglove with a shake of his head.

"Why not?" asked Laurel.

"It's pretty wild," replied the pixie. "And dangerous."

Laurel studied Foxglove. "Well, I won't be alone. I'll be with you."

Foxglove thought for a moment. "All right," he said. "We'll do it. But just a short trip. And not too far into the forest."

Laurel agreed. So the two explorers set off immediately.

Their path took them along the edge of the Dappled Woods. As they walked, Foxglove asked about the neat, lovely gardens he saw here and there. And Laurel asked Foxglove what plants she might see in the Great Forest.

In an hour's time, they came to the end of the fairy woods. Laurel stopped and stared in wonder at the strange forest outside. Old, twisted tree branches met overhead, blocking out the sun. Thick vines coiled around tree trunks and tumbled across the path.

"Do you still want to do this?" asked Foxglove.

Laurel gulped. She wondered what she was getting herself into. But she straightened her wings.

"Let's go," she said.

Laurel and Foxglove crossed over into the wild, tangled forest.

CHAPTER FOUR

Scavenging in the Great Forest

verything was much darker in the Great Forest. Laurel tripped over a vine that stretched across the path. A thorn caught at her sleeve, and she stopped to pull it loose.

"This forest certainly has been left in a mess," she said.

"Forests are supposed to be this way," replied Foxglove as he swept some brush aside.

"Are you saying that the Dappled Woods isn't natural?"

"It's nice, Laurel. Neat and pretty," said Foxglove. "But it's *not* natural."

Laurel was about to object when a loud cawing sounded nearby. It was followed by a strange snort and then a high squeal.

Laurel shivered. She couldn't understand these animals clearly. What were they like? Were they dangerous?

As they rounded a sharp curve, Laurel noticed something sparkling between two tree branches. It was a spider-web that was at least two fairy wingspans wide. Laurel had never seen a web so huge—or so beautiful.

At the center of the web sat a shiny black spider. "Oh, look!" Laurel exclaimed, reaching out.

"Don't touch it!" warned Foxglove. "It's poisonous. If it bites you, you'll be in trouble."

"The spiders out here bite?" asked Laurel in alarm.

"Lots of things out here bite," warned Foxglove. "Don't touch anything that I don't touch."

That sounded like good advice. So Laurel watched Foxglove carefully. She turned where he turned and ducked where he ducked. Foxglove's warnings frightened her a little. At the same time, she was excited. She was seeing sights that no other fairy had ever seen.

And what strange sights they were! A moss green lizard slithered up a tree. A gold-and-black snake slipped across the path. Brilliantly colored birds flitted from branch to branch. The creatures in the Dappled Woods seemed small and tame by comparison.

Suddenly Foxglove paused and sniffed the air carefully. His nose crinkled.

"Do you smell something awful?" he asked.

Laurel sniffed. The air was full of the scents of plants and flowers. Many of the smells were new to her. But none seemed awful.

"No," she said. "Everything smells wonderful to me."

"Maybe it's just my imagination," said Foxglove. But he sounded worried.

As they moved on, Laurel reminded herself why they'd come. She began to search for something to scavenge. The first thing she noticed was a large, empty snail shell. A color-ful pattern covered the shell from end to end.

"Look!" she called to Foxglove. "I've found just the thing

for you!"

"A snail shell?" grumbled Foxglove. "I don't think so."

"Why not? I've never seen one this big."

"Well, I have. We use them as shoe scrapers and doorstops. I need something special to take back."

Next Laurel found a huge set of antlers. But Foxglove wasn't interested in that either.

"Afraid not," said the pixie, shaking his head. "Everyone I know has a set. We use them for coatracks."

He also quickly turned down a piece of wood shaped like a bird, a spotted mushroom, and a sky blue stone.

"Well, fine," muttered Laurel as she dropped the stone. This scavenging business was tougher than she'd imagined. And Foxglove was a lot harder to please than she'd dreamed.

Even so, Laurel found herself respecting the pixie for his knowledge. He showed Laurel how to get through thick brush without having to fly. He pointed out which berries were safe and which were poisonous. He told her the names of plants and animals she'd never seen before. He certainly knew his way around the forest.

After a while, Foxglove stopped and sniffed the air again.

"Are you sure you don't smell something bad?" he asked with a frown.

Laurel sniffed the air. For just a moment, she caught a hint of something unpleasant. But then it was gone.

"No," she said. "Not really."

"I don't like it," said Foxglove. "I think we should go back."

"We can't go back. Not yet. Not until we've scavenged something," replied Laurel.

Foxglove gave another worried glance to both sides. But he went on.

Before long Laurel realized that the forest was becoming brighter. The trees were smaller and farther apart. Suddenly, around the next turn, the trees almost disappeared. Clumps of low bushes separated them from the largest open space Laurel had ever seen.

"Oh, my," she gasped.

This meadow was ten times as big as the Ancient Clearing in the Dappled Woods. Long grasses waved in the breeze. Wildflowers of many shades grew everywhere.

"How beautiful," Laurel said, stepping forward.

"Don't go out in the open!" Foxglove cried sharply. "Stay at the edge by the bushes."

So they walked along the meadow's edge. Laurel peered around in excitement. She spotted some familiar creatures hopping through the grass.

"Rabbits!" she exclaimed.

"This is New Warren, where the rabbits live," Foxglove said. Pointing to their right, he said, "Old Warren, where we pixies live, is off in that direction."

Foxglove stopped and looked around. Suddenly he announced, "The tour's over. It's time to go back."

"What? But why?" Laurel asked. Then she saw that Foxglove looked truly worried. And with her next breath, she realized—

"What an awful smell!" she exclaimed.

"So you finally smell it?" said Foxglove. "Well, that's why we've got to go."

"But we haven't found anything for you to scavenge yet," said Laurel.

Foxglove pointed to a spot several feet in front of them. Laurel could clearly see the trail of some wild creature. The grass was torn, and wildflowers had been ripped up. Large footprints marked the soft ground.

"What kind of footprints are those?" Laurel asked.

"You don't want to know," said Foxglove. "Now let's—"

There was a loud crash from the woods.

The pixie spun about and peered in the direction of the noise. "Oh no," he whispered. Then, with wild fear in his eyes, he turned to Laurel.

"Hide!" he hissed.

CHAPTER FIVE

Danger in the Meadow

oxglove quickly crawled under a bush, pulling Laurel after him.

"Keep quiet!" he ordered. "And don't let him see you!"

"Who?" asked Laurel. "Who's out there?"

"Quiet, I said! And stay flat." Foxglove pushed Laurel down and flattened himself against the ground too.

Laurel kept quiet. But she edged forward a little to see what was going on.

The meadow was empty. All the rabbits seemed to have vanished into their holes. Yet Laurel still couldn't see who had frightened them and Foxglove so.

But the noise was getting louder and closer. It was a horrible, thundering, stomping sound. The creature must be big—or angry, Laurel thought. Or both.

And the awful smell grew stronger by the minute.

Then Laurel saw the creature. Or at least part of him. The bush still blocked most of Laurel's view. But she got an unpleasantly close look at the creature's feet. They were huge and gray and covered with tufts of black hair. His long, sharp toenails curved under like claws.

The creature paused not far from Laurel and Foxglove. They heard a deep grunt and a snort. Then he sniffed. Three loud, long sniffs.

The feet slowly turned. Now they were pointed toward the bush where Laurel and Foxglove lay hidden.

"Oh no!" whispered Laurel. "I think he smells us!"

"Quiet!" hissed Foxglove.

Then...

Stomp, stomp, stomp. The creature thundered toward them. The ground shook harder as every step brought him nearer.

Laurel was shaking too. She pressed her wings against her back. She wanted to shut her eyes. But she couldn't keep herself from looking.

The awful feet came closer. Laurel thought the creature was going to walk right over her. But he stopped just in front of the bush.

The smell was horrible. Laurel was afraid she would sneeze or cough. But she didn't dare move—not even to hold her nose.

She heard rustling right above her. The creature was parting the branches with his hands. Laurel wondered how long it would be before he looked down.

But he never did. The big hairy feet turned away.

Stomp, stomp, stomp. The creature went back across the meadow, the same way he'd come. Gradually the footsteps grew fainter. But neither Laurel nor Foxglove moved for several long minutes.

Finally Foxglove sat up. He looked pale and frightened. Laurel sat up too.

"What was that?" she gasped.

"A troll," Foxglove replied.

"But...but...there's no such thing as trolls," stammered Laurel. "They're just stories."

"Oh! Well! I do beg your pardon," exclaimed Foxglove. "We must have imagined the whole thing! No nasty smell, no thundering feet, no troll!"

"Well, I've heard of trolls," Laurel said. "But the woodfairy elders always said they were only make-believe."

Foxglove snorted. "I'm starting to understand why woodfairies never leave the Dappled Woods. No common sense!"

Laurel frowned. But she really couldn't blame Foxglove for being upset.

Finally she asked, "What would he have done if he'd caught us?"

"Who knows?" replied Foxglove. "Those who do get caught never escape to tell what happened."

Laurel gulped. "It's lucky he didn't have a very good sense of smell."

"Oh, trolls have an excellent sense of smell," replied Foxglove. "It's just that they smell so bad themselves, they have a hard time smelling anything else."

"Are there a lot of trolls in this part of the forest?" asked Laurel with a shiver.

"No," said Foxglove. "I've never even been this close to one before. There's a wide river between here and their home in the Bog of Bleak. Trolls hate deep, rushing water, so they usually never cross the river. But when they do, they take anything—and anyone—they want."

Foxglove nervously glanced over each shoulder. "Now can we turn around?" he asked.

Laurel nodded. It was late afternoon, and the sun would be setting soon. She certainly didn't want to run into a troll again, especially in the dark.

The woodfairy and the pixie started back through the thick forest. They went more slowly than before. But now they weren't looking for things to scavenge. They were too busy listening, watching, and sniffing for trolls.

Finally they reached the edge of the Dappled Woods. From there they hurried back to Laurel's treehouse. They found both Chitters and Mistletoe waiting for them.

"Where were you, Laurel?" asked the little mouse.

"Why don't you both come up with me? I'll tell you all about it," replied Laurel.

She turned and looked at Foxglove. The pixie seemed to be as tired and hungry as she was.

"I've got plenty to eat," she said. "Do you think you could…?"

"Climb up?" said Foxglove. "Sure, why not? After what we've been through, a treetop doesn't seem that scary."

Laurel flew up to her treehouse as Mistletoe and Chitters scrambled along beside her. They stood on the porch and watched Foxglove. The pixie climbed slowly and carefully, never looking down. But he made it to the top.

Laurel went inside. She filled bowls with bread, mushrooms, and blueberries. Then she made a big pot of tea from tender ferns and violets.

She served dinner on the porch. While they ate, Laurel told Mistletoe and Chitters about her adventure.

Foxglove listened carefully to Laurel and the animals. It

wasn't long before he understood enough to join in.

"Dangerous!" trilled Chitters. "I'd never go there! Not me!"

"It *is* dangerous," said Mistletoe softly. "And I told you I thought something was wrong out there."

"Don't worry," Laurel said. "I don't think I'll be leaving the Dappled Woods again for a long while."

"At least not alone," said Foxglove firmly.

By the time they all finished eating, it had grown quite dark. Laurel lit a small lantern.

In the dim light, Laurel noticed a big tear in the pixie's cloak. A piece of cloth was nearly ready to fall off.

"Foxglove," she said, "your cloak is ruined."

"Not at all," replied Foxglove. "Just a little tear. And I can use the torn piece for the quilt I'm making."

"Quilt?" asked Mistletoe. "What's a quilt?"

Foxglove explained that the pixies saved scraps of cloth to stitch together for blankets. Pixies never threw anything away. They used whatever they had until it crumbled into dust.

"Woodfairies don't make quilts," said Laurel. "We weave new cloth for our blankets and clothes. Oh, we mend them sometimes. But when they wear out, we don't keep them."

"What do you do with them then?" asked Foxglove.

"We bury them," explained Laurel. "So they rot and become part of the soil. We try to use only things that can go back to the soil."

Foxglove thought this over. "That sounds like a good idea," he said at last.

"So does making quilts," said Laurel.

Laurel, Foxglove, and the two animals looked out over the Dappled Woods. The darkness deepened. Lanterns came on here and there. Soon Mistletoe and Chitters settled down in a corner and fell asleep.

But Laurel and Foxglove continued to talk quietly. Laurel told about her lessons and how worried she was about her contribution to the Celebration. Foxglove told about pixie life. And he answered question after question about the world outside the Dappled Woods.

"Who else lives out there?" Laurel asked.

Foxglove told her about the sturdy dwarves who lived in the mountains. And about the many wild animals who made their homes in the forest. He didn't add anything else about the trolls. They'd both had enough of that subject for one day.

The two sat for a while in comfortable silence. Far below they could see a circle of lights around the Ancient Clearing.

"Tell me something," said Foxglove finally. "Is the Crystal as beautiful on the inside as it is on the outside?"

"Oh, yes! It's glorious," whispered Laurel. "It shines with the light of hundreds of tiny crystals."

"I'd love to see that," said Foxglove in a soft voice.

Laurel made a quick decision. "You *will* see it," she said. "Because you'll be here for the Celebration."

Foxglove's mouth dropped open. "You mean I can stay for a while?" he asked. "And meet the other fairies?"

"Yes," answered Laurel.

Laurel was surprised at her own words. But everything that had happened that day made her see things in a new way. The woodfairies knew so little about the world around them.

A world that Laurel now realized was filled with dangers and wonders.

Laurel knew that woodfairies didn't belong out in the Great Forest. Even so, they shouldn't pretend that it didn't exist.

So she'd offer part of that world to the fairies. She'd show them Foxglove.

~

The next morning, Laurel had a hard time waking up. She and Foxglove had talked late into the night. And the excitement of her adventure had kept her awake after the pixie left.

She yawned and thought about going back to sleep. But then she decided she should practice her flute some more.

Laurel got up, dressed, and went out to her porch. She was about to raise her flute to her lips when she heard voices. They were coming from the clearing. And they sounded upset.

Laurel glided down from her treehouse and over to the hollow by the waterfall. "Foxglove?" she called.

Chitters appeared from behind a rock. "Not here!" the little chipmunk reported.

"Oh? Where is he?"

"Not here," Chitters chattered. "Just not here."

"What's going on in the clearing?" Laurel asked.

"Don't know," Chitters said. "Lots of fairy folk running around. Not safe to stick my nose in. Not safe at all!"

"Oh no," Laurel breathed. "I'll bet it's Foxglove. He must have wandered over there. And the other fairies found him."

She sighed. "Well, I said he could meet them. So I'd better make sure things are going all right."

Laurel hurried to the clearing. But there was no sign of Foxglove. Instead, she saw many fairies fluttering wildly

about. They were crying, "It's gone! It's gone!"

"What's gone?" Laurel asked.

But none of them would stop fluttering and crying. Laurel couldn't even get Ivy to talk to her.

Then Laurel noticed the elders. They were all gathered around the tree stump where the Crystal was kept. Laurel could hear the unhappiness in their soft voices.

"What's happened?" Laurel asked. "What's wrong?"

The elders moved aside so Laurel could see the tree stump. The door was open, and—

The Crystal of the Chronicles was gone!

CHAPTER SIX

The Stolen Crystal

aurel gasped. "Where is it? Where's the Crystal?"

"Missing!" sighed all the elders in one breath.

"But how?" asked Laurel.

"We don't know," moaned Ivy. "It just vanished!"

"I'm afraid it didn't simply vanish," said Mistress Marigold. "It's been stolen."

All the fairies turned toward Mistress Marigold. They stared at her in surprise.

"Stolen?" repeated one fairy. "But who stole it? And where is it now? And what should we do?"

Primrose stepped forward. She crossed her arms and announced, "I know what has to be done. We must search everyone's house."

"Don't be silly, child," said Mistress Gooseberry in her usual cross voice. "The Crystal couldn't have been stolen by a woodfairy."

"It doesn't make sense," agreed Mistress Marigold.

"Why not?" asked Primrose.

"Because the Crystal belongs to all of us," explained Mistress Marigold. "You can't steal something that's already yours. So it must have been taken by someone it doesn't belong to—an outsider."

"But who?" said another fairy.

"I think I've found a clue!" called Mistress Gooseberry. She'd been looking around the base of the stump. "Whoever took the Crystal left this behind." She held up a scrap of greenish brown cloth.

The other fairies rushed to look. All except Laurel, who didn't have to. She already knew that she'd seen this bit of cloth before. It was part of Foxglove's cloak!

But why would the scrap be here? What had Foxglove been doing in the clearing?

An elder who was a weaver studied the scrap. "Well, it's certainly not fairy cloth," she said.

"I could tell that," said Mistress Gooseberry sourly. "But what is it?"

"It's not badly woven, but the cloth is rough. And in this color, it must have been made by..." The fairy weaver thought hard, as if trying to remember something from long ago. "By a pixie! Yes. I believe that this is a scrap of pixie cloth."

"A pixie?" one fairy asked. "But they never come here, do they?"

"Not often," said Mistress Marigold. "But it has happened."

"I saw one once," said Mistress Gooseberry. "And he—I think it was a he—was horribly dirty! He was drinking from the stream at the edge of the woods. He made nasty slurping sounds. Luckily I was able to hurry away before he saw me."

"So does that mean a pixie stole the Crystal?" Ivy asked slowly.

Laurel couldn't keep silent any longer. "I don't believe that pixies steal," she said to the others. "They scavenge. It's a totally different thing."

"Oh? Since when do you know so much about pixies?"

asked Primrose.

Before Laurel could answer, the other young woodfairies began talking. They kept asking the elders what could be done. The elders sadly announced that nothing could be done. The Crystal had been stolen, and they wouldn't be able to get it back. There would be no more Celebrations, no more readings of the Chronicles.

"How sad," said Ivy in a low voice. "Life in the Dappled Woods will never be the same!"

"But something *can* be done," said Laurel. "We'll track down the thief. Then we'll bring back the Crystal."

"Track down?" said Primrose.

"Bring back?" said Ivy.

"Whatever gave you such a silly idea?" snorted Mistress Gooseberry. "It's much too dangerous to go outside the Dappled Woods for any reason. Even for the Crystal."

"Well, I'm not afraid to go outside," said Laurel. "I'll try to find the Crystal—if someone will come with me."

The other fairies nervously flapped their wings.

Mistress Gooseberry stepped forward. "Absolutely not, Laurel," she said. "No one will go with you because *you're* not going. We must simply accept what has happened and try to get on with our lives. Now I suggest that we all go home."

The fairies looked at each other. Then, with soft farewells, they started to leave the clearing.

Laurel turned to Mistress Marigold. "Please," she begged. "Stop them. Get them to listen."

But her teacher just shook her head. "I can't, Laurel. They're not ready to hear."

Mistress Marigold gave Laurel a little hug. Then she turned away and headed home.

Only Ivy remained in the clearing now. She stared at Laurel with a puzzled look on her face.

"Would you really go outside the Dappled Woods?" she asked.

"Well, somebody's got to," said Laurel. "Otherwise, we've lost the most important part of fairy life. Lost it forever. Won't you come with me, Ivy?"

"Oh, Laurel, I would if I could. Honestly, I would. But whenever I even think about leaving the Dappled Woods, I...I get dizzy. I just can't do it. But it was brave of you to suggest it."

Laurel sighed. She didn't feel brave. If she were truly brave, she'd go all by herself.

"Cheer up, Laurel," Ivy said softly. "At least you don't have to worry about playing your flute now." Ivy smiled sadly. Then she said good-bye.

Tired and upset, Laurel set out for her own treehouse. All the way there, she thought about what had happened.

Yet exactly what *had* happened? Though she hadn't known Foxglove long, Laurel trusted him. She knew he'd never steal the Crystal.

But the piece of cloth meant that Foxglove had been in the clearing. Maybe he knew who had taken the Crystal. Should she tell the other fairies about him?

No, she didn't dare. They'd never believe that he hadn't stolen the Crystal. And they still wouldn't leave the Dappled Woods to go after it. They'd just be mad at her for making friends with a pixie.

By the time Laurel reached home, she'd made a decision. She had to do something about the missing Crystal. Why? Because she *could*. Unlike Ivy, she could go outside the Dappled Woods. She already had.

Laurel also knew where the pixies lived. Or at least she knew the general direction. If Foxglove had gone home, she could follow him. Maybe he'd help her find the thief.

"No more thinking," Laurel told herself. "It's time to go."

Quickly she gathered some food and water. Then she put everything into her bag. For a moment, she thought about leaving her flute behind. But it seemed so friendly and familiar. She decided to take it along after all. Something from home would give her courage.

Finally she changed into her oldest dress. "Well," she said aloud, "I'm ready."

But she didn't move. Her knees began to shake. If she was going to go at all, she knew she had to leave that very minute.

Laurel glided to the ground. With one last look at her beloved home and Thunder Falls, she turned away. And she headed straight for the forest.

Laurel didn't stop until she reached the edge of the Dappled Woods. There she paused and stared straight ahead. The forest seemed darker than it had before. The trees appeared taller and the vines more twisted.

Then something caught Laurel's eye. It was a scrap of greenish brown cloth hanging from a branch. She quickly grabbed it.

"Foxglove!" she whispered. "It's another piece from his cloak. He must have come this way!"

CHAPTER SEVEN

On the Trail

aurel was surprised that Foxglove had lost another part of his cloak. It seemed strange that he'd lost two pieces in one day. And he hadn't stopped to pick up either one. What would he use to make his quilt?

Laurel shook her head. Something didn't make sense. She'd just have to keep her eyes open and try to figure this out.

Laurel took a deep breath and then stepped onto the twisting path. She remembered to turn where Foxglove had turned and to duck where he had ducked. She realized that he'd taught her a lot about getting along in the forest.

Still Laurel felt lonely and frightened. If only—

"Laurel! Laurel! Wait for me," called a soft voice. It came from the underbrush.

Laurel spun around. "Mistletoe!" she cried.

Before the mouse could reply, Chitters dashed into sight.

"What are you two doing here?" Laurel asked.

"We heard that the Crystal is missing—along with Foxglove. And we figured you'd try to find both of them. Well, we're not going to let you search all by yourself," said Mistletoe bravely.

"Absolutely not!" said Chitters. "Out of the question! Don't even think about it!"

"You can't come along," Laurel said firmly. "This is my problem, not yours."

Mistletoe shook her head. "You're our friend," she said. "So your problems are our problems. And we know at least some of the paths through the Great Forest. Besides, we care about Foxglove too."

"Absolutely," added Chitters.

Laurel started to object again. But then she thought things over. Her animal friends were right. And to be honest, Laurel was happy to see them. Now she wouldn't be in this strange place all by herself.

"All right," she said slowly. Then she smiled. "And thanks. I'm glad you're here."

"Let's go," said Chitters. "Forward and onward!"

Mistletoe immediately took the lead. Laurel and Chitters followed the little mouse along the twisting trail. To Laurel, the forest seemed quieter than it had before. All along the trail, she saw broken and twisted branches. She was sure they hadn't been that way yesterday. But she told herself to stop imagining things.

Then Laurel noticed something hanging from a twisted vine. It was another scrap of cloth. She stopped and took it in her hand.

"Foxglove couldn't have torn his cloak so many times by accident," she announced. "He must have done it on purpose."

"Why?" asked Chitters.

"To leave a trail, of course," said Laurel.

"But why leave a trail of torn cloth?" replied Mistletoe.

"Surely he knew we could follow his scent."

"You can smell that Foxglove came this way?" asked Laurel.

"Yes," said the mouse. "He went down this path just a few hours ago. Can't you tell?"

Laurel shook her head. "No. I can't smell a thing."

"There," said Chitters with satisfaction. "We can help. No doubt about it. Absolutely! Positively!"

"But he's leaving a trail that even I can follow," Laurel said, fingering the piece of cloth. "Which means he must want me to follow him. Now what does that tell us?"

The answer to her own question popped into Laurel's mind. "Foxglove must have seen someone take the Crystal!" she exclaimed. "He's tracking the thief. And he's showing me which way he went."

Then Laurel thought about all the broken twigs and branches along the path. She realized that Mistletoe must be having the same unpleasant thoughts.

"Mistletoe," she asked. "Do you smell anything else along this trail?"

"Yes," said the mouse quietly. "But I didn't want to bring it up."

"What is it?" asked Laurel.

"I think it might be a troll!" whispered Mistletoe.

"A troll?" gasped Chitters. "Absolutely not! Out of the question! Don't even think about it!"

Laurel turned to Mistletoe. "Can you tell if Foxglove and the troll came along this path at the same time?"

Mistletoe sniffed the ground carefully. "The troll was here first. Foxglove came later."

"So Foxglove is following a troll," said Laurel slowly.

"And the troll must be the thief who took the Crystal. Foxglove told me that trolls steal anything they want. I'll bet Foxglove is trying to get the Crystal back. And he left a trail so I could help him!"

She stopped and looked at her friends. "This is going to be even more dangerous than I thought," she warned them.

Mistletoe spoke quickly. "That means we'll just have to be more careful."

"Absolutely," Chitters whispered, glancing nervously about.

"I know," said Laurel softly.

The mouse put her nose down on the path and sniffed deeply. Then she headed off, with Laurel and Chitters close behind.

Mistletoe's nose told her that Foxglove hadn't always stayed on the path. Sometimes the mouse tracked the pixie into the underbrush. Chitters could usually follow her, but not Laurel. Once or twice, the woodfairy had to use her wings to keep up with her friends.

Finally Laurel and the animals reached the meadow where the rabbits lived. Everything was still and silent. No breeze rustled the long grasses or swayed the wildflowers. There wasn't a single rabbit in sight.

Chitters sat up and wiggled his nose. "Something's wrong! Definitely wrong!"

Mistletoe sniffed too. "A troll was here. And not very long ago."

"How about Foxglove?" Laurel asked.

"He's been here too," Mistletoe said. The mouse raced along the edge of the meadow. "Foxglove went this way," she announced.

Sure enough, Laurel soon spotted another scrap of cloth hanging from a bush. She and her friends circled the meadow, keeping a sharp eye out for trolls.

At the far edge of the grassy space, Mistletoe dashed into the forest again. The others followed. For a long time, they walked in silence. Then Mistletoe paused and made a horrible face.

"A troll has been here recently," she said. "In fact, it smells like he might still be nearby!"

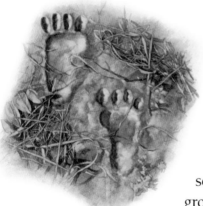

Laurel noticed that several large branches had been broken and tossed aside. And huge footprints were everywhere.

"A troll has been here, all right," Laurel said. "More than one troll, from the looks of things."

Laurel saw a handful of cloth scraps scattered about. Marks on the ground showed that something had been dragged away.

Suddenly it all made sense. "Foxglove must have been captured!" exclaimed Laurel. "By trolls!"

"Captured?" Chitters squeaked.

Laurel's heart beat wildly. But there was never any doubt about what she was going to do. "I've got to save him!" she cried.

She marched into the woods, following the trail of the trolls.

The two animals waited for a moment. Then they charged after Laurel. Mistletoe called, "Wait, Laurel! Please, you have to be careful! Slow down—"

But Laurel was too wrapped up in her own thoughts to pay attention. "Who knows what those trolls will do to Foxglove? If I don't free him fast, they might—"

With a great whoosh, Laurel's feet suddenly jerked out from under her. Head over heels she went, straight up into the air.

CHAPTER EIGHT

Trapped!

or a minute, the world spun around and around and up and down.

At last the bobbing stopped. Laurel caught her breath and tried to figure out what had happened. She was hanging in midair and could feel tight cords surrounding her. By moving her head a little, she saw a bit of webbing.

"A net!" she said. "Someone set a trap!"

Laurel turned her head a little farther. She spotted something else hanging nearby. At first it looked like a bundle of fur and ears. Then Laurel realized that it was another net. Chitters was trapped inside! But Mistletoe was nowhere to be seen.

"Are you all right?" Laurel called to the chipmunk. "Where is Mistletoe?"

"I'm here on the ground," the mouse called back. "I'll see if I can help you."

Laurel pulled at the net. "We've got to get down from here before—"

Too late! Wild shouts rang out through the forest. Mistletoe quickly disappeared into the thick underbrush.

Three trolls sprang onto the trail. Laurel had never seen an entire troll before. The sight was more frightening than she'd ever imagined.

The trolls were huge. Their arms and legs were nearly as

thick as tree branches. And the creatures were monstrous! Clawlike fingernails sprouted from their hands, while long teeth jutted from their mouths.

The trolls gathered below the nets, laughing deep, gruff laughs. The biggest troll turned to the others and growled something. Laurel tried to hear. It was so hard to understand them!

But the longer Laurel listened, the more she understood. Soon she could make out almost everything they said.

"More for the feast," the big troll said. "Bring them!"

The other trolls bent down and cut some ropes. Laurel fell through the air and landed in the arms of a troll, net and all.

Then the big troll cut down the net that held Chitters. Meanwhile, a troll bent down to pick up Laurel's bag. Suddenly he cursed and grabbed at something in the grass. Laurel caught sight of Mistletoe's tail. Luckily the little mouse slipped through the troll's fingers. She vanished into a clump of bushes.

"Fool!" bellowed the big troll. "Find it!"

The trolls searched for the mouse for several minutes. At last their leader called them back.

"Enough! A good mouthful gone. Try explaining *that* to the king. See how hard he laughs."

The other two trolls suddenly looked nervous.

"Move!" the big troll ordered.

One of the smaller trolls threw Laurel over his shoulder. She cast a worried glance at Chitters. The tiny chipmunk was gnawing at his net. But the thick webbing was too hard for him to chew through.

In spite of their size, the trolls moved quickly. Laurel bumped and bounced against the troll's back as he marched along. That was unpleasant, but even worse was the stink coming from the troll.

It was much later when Laurel heard a rushing sound in the distance. The sound grew louder and louder. Finally the trolls stopped.

Laurel twisted around and saw that they'd reached a wide river. She remembered that Foxglove had mentioned it. A river that separated the trolls' land from the rest of the forest. Foxglove had said that the trolls usually didn't cross it. Their fear of deep, rushing water kept them away. Or at least it used to. What had happened to change that?

The troll carrying Laurel turned a bit. Now Laurel saw that a large tree lay across the river. Dirt covered its long roots. The tree must have fallen in a recent storm.

Looking closer, Laurel noted that several ropes held the tree in place. The trolls had tied it down so they could use it as a bridge. So this was why they were going so far from their bog!

The trolls stared at the rushing water uneasily.

"Go on, you!" the one carrying Laurel said. He pushed the troll who was carrying Chitters.

The other snarled and angrily pushed back. "Not me!"

A bit of hope stirred in Laurel's heart. Maybe they'd be too frightened to cross.

But the big troll quickly stepped in. "Move!" he barked. "Scared of the river, you two? Move now or find out what 'scared' really means."

The two smaller trolls muttered. But they began marching toward the bridge.

The troll carrying Laurel started across. The fallen tree wasn't very steady. The river tugged at its branches. And the

weight of Laurel and the troll made it wobble even more.

The troll moved along slowly. He bent over so he could keep one hand on the log. When they reached the other side, he grunted happily. His friends soon followed.

On this side of the river, the ground was wet and muddy. The trees were short and twisted, and there wasn't a flower to be seen anywhere. Laurel thought that it was a horrible, ugly place. Yet the trolls seemed happy to be back.

"Right! Get moving," growled the leader.

Once more they set off, Laurel and Chitters still in the nets. It was slower going as they entered the bog. In some spots, pools of dirty water covered the trail.

The smell of the water made Laurel's head spin. Now she understood where the trolls' awful stink came from.

Finally the trolls waded to some higher ground in the bog. The troll carrying Laurel grunted and threw her down. The other troll dropped Chitters beside her.

Laurel sputtered and sat up. She was still caught in the net. But at least she could take a good look at the troll village.

The sight didn't make her feel any better. All around her stood miserable little huts made of sticks and mud. Smoky campfires burned here and there. And wooden cages hung from posts and trees.

The big troll called out, "Ho! A surprise for the feast!"

At once trolls poured out of the low doorways. There were several mothers with babies. And a few young trolls. Most of the others seemed to be hunters, like the ones who had captured Laurel and Chitters.

Now all the trolls gathered around. One poked Laurel with his foot. "Huge bird, that one is," he grunted. "Stupid prize, Fang. What's it for?"

The big troll frowned. "You's the stupid one, Mold," he said. "Never seen a woodfairy?"

There was a confused muttering from the trolls. Laurel pulled away as more trolls poked at her with clawed fingers and toes.

Mold shook his head. "Faw! What's the use of this one?"

Fang curled his lip. Suddenly he reached out and picked up Laurel's bag. "Got stuff!" he shouted at Mold.

Fang opened the bag and dumped everything out. He gave the bag a quick sniff and threw it to the ground. Then he pawed through Laurel's belongings.

Laurel caught her breath as Fang grabbed her flute. He clearly didn't know what it was. He licked it, gnawed on one end, then tapped it on the ground.

"Oh no," whispered Laurel. She was certain that Fang would smash the flute to pieces. But the troll only shrugged and tossed it aside. It landed on the ground near Laurel.

Then Fang took the cork out of Laurel's water gourd and sniffed. "Fresh!" he snorted. He poured the water onto the ground.

Meanwhile, Mold dug into Laurel's food. He studied the biscuits and berries. Then he mashed them together and stuffed the crumbs and juice into his mouth.

Mold chewed for a moment. Soon an angry frown crossed his face. He spat out the mouthful and stepped on it for good measure. Grabbing Fang's arm, he growled, "Try to poison me, would you?"

Fang pulled away. "Get off!" he roared. "Who asked you to eat it?"

The trolls started to fight. As they pushed and shouted, Laurel carefully reached out and grabbed her flute and bag. Quickly she hid them under her cloak. Then she glanced around, looking for some way to escape. Could she struggle out of the net and fly off above the trolls' heads? If so, where would she go? To the treetops? Could trolls climb trees?

Her eyes fell on Chitters. How could she free both of them without the trolls noticing?

The fight was over as fast as it had started. Fang knocked Mold to the ground.

"My stuff, Mold! And my prisoners, hear? Least till the king gets here."

At that, Fang snatched up the nets that held Laurel and Chitters. He dragged his prisoners to the hanging cages. Into one large cage, he tossed Laurel. He slammed the door shut and locked it with an iron key.

Fang moved to a smaller cage. Into this one went Chitters. Then Fang and the other trolls headed back to the campfires.

As Laurel freed herself from the net, she looked over at the cage that held Chitters. The chipmunk was also working himself out of his net.

"What do we do now?" Laurel whispered.

Chitters looked around. "Wait for help?" he suggested.

Laurel shook her head sadly. Who could help them?

"We'll wait until nightfall," she whispered back. "Then we'll look for a way out. It's too dangerous until then—"

Rustling leaves in a corner of her cage drew Laurel's attention. She stared fearfully as the mound of leaves moved.

Suddenly a creature popped out. It yawned, blinked its eyes in the light, and shook off a few leaves.

"Foxglove!" Laurel cried.

"Laurel!" called Foxglove joyfully.

The woodfairy and the pixie hugged. Then Foxglove seemed to realize what had happened.

"Oh no!" he gasped. "They caught you too!"

"I'm afraid so—and Chitters. Mistletoe got away. But who knows what will happen to her alone in the forest. Oh, Foxglove, we're in a terrible mess!"

"And it's all my fault," moaned Foxglove. "I shouldn't have left that trail for you to follow. We'll never get out of this place."

"Don't talk that way," said Laurel. "You were right to leave a trail. And we'll get out of here—somehow. But how did you get caught? What happened?"

"Well, after I left your treehouse, I went back to my hollow. But I couldn't sleep. I was too excited about meeting the other woodfairies. So I decided to take a walk. Then, at the edge of the Ancient Clearing, I smelled a troll. I hid behind a tree just as one came by.

"The troll spotted the doors in the stump and went straight for it. You should have seen how he laughed when he found the Crystal! Then he tossed it into his bag and hurried away.

"I decided to follow him. I figured I could outsmart him and take the Crystal back. But a bunch of his troll pals joined him, and they caught me.

"Now they've got you too. Thanks to me," he finished sadly.

"It's not your fault, Foxglove," Laurel told him. "And between the two of us, we'll think of a way out of here."

They were interrupted by a new band of trolls coming in from the woods. A group gathered near the cages, grunting and growling at one another. Laurel and Foxglove listened carefully.

"I can't understand everything they're saying," whispered Foxglove.

Laurel shook her head. "I can. And it's not good," she whispered back. "In fact, we'd better get out of here as soon as we can!"

"What's up?" asked Foxglove.

"Their king is arriving tonight. When he gets here, there's supposed to be a big feast. And—oh, Foxglove, I'm pretty sure that Chitters is on the menu!"

But Laurel and Foxglove couldn't think of a way to escape. All they could do was watch and listen.

After a while, they noticed that Fang seemed to be in charge. As trolls arrived, he quickly put them to work. Some began setting up rough wooden tables and chairs.

Other trolls dragged in a huge, ugly throne made from logs. They placed the throne in the center of the village. Next they smoothed the muddy earth nearby. Finally they placed a dirty, ragged rug in front of the throne.

Fang eyed their work. At last he nodded and barked another order.

One by one, the trolls stepped forward. And one by one, they emptied their bags and nets into a huge pile on the rug. Out tumbled golden necklaces and silver chains. Thick bracelets and jeweled boxes. Heaps of coins and enormous gemstones.

Laurel wondered who could have made these treasures. Not the woodfairies. And absolutely, certainly, and definitely not the trolls.

Suddenly Laurel saw something that made her heart jump into her throat. Another troll was emptying his bag onto the pile. Out fell a large, glittering stone.

It was the Crystal of the Chronicles!

A Beastly Feast

he Crystal!" exclaimed Laurel, grabbing hold of the bars of the cage.

The troll heard her cry. He laughed and picked up the Crystal. Then, looking at Laurel, he placed the sparkling object on top of the pile. "Easy pickings!" he shouted.

Laurel sank back to the floor of the cage. "We have to get out of here," she moaned. "And we have to get the Crystal."

Foxglove put a hand on Laurel's shoulder. "We will," he said. But he didn't sound as if he believed his own words.

The long, horrible day continued. Fang brought a young troll over to see his catch. The little troll peered at Laurel and Foxglove curiously. Then he poked a stick through the cage bars, narrowly missing Foxglove.

"No," grunted Fang as he grabbed the stick. "Save them for the king." He dragged the little troll off to one of the huts.

Later Mold walked by and gave the cage a quick push to set it swinging.

"Dance!" he laughed as Laurel and Foxglove tumbled from one side to the other.

But for the most part, the three prisoners were left alone. The trolls knew they couldn't escape. And there was still much to prepare for the king's feast. Laurel watched as they filled huge pitchers with water dipped right out of the bog. They also placed baskets of food on the rough tables.

"Look at what they're going to eat," whispered Laurel to Foxglove. "Rotten berries. Moldy acorns. Muddy leaves."

"And those are poisonous," added Foxglove. He pointed to the mushrooms one troll was carrying. "But not to trolls, I guess."

Meanwhile, the treasure pile in front of the throne grew higher and higher.

"Who made all those wonderful things?" Laurel asked Foxglove.

"Not trolls, you can be sure of that," Foxglove replied. "I don't think they make anything nice. They just steal it. They probably took most of this from the dwarves. They're the ones who make things from metals like gold and silver. I think the trolls even stole the locks on our cages from the dwarves."

Laurel couldn't stop staring at the treasures. Until lately, she hadn't given much thought to those who lived outside the Dappled Woods. Now she longed to meet the dwarves and learn more about them. But she already knew quite enough about trolls.

Darkness crept over the bog. A huge bonfire shot smoke and ashes into the dull gray sky. The trolls gathered around the fire as if waiting for something.

Soon a low, steady sound caught Laurel's ear.

"Listen!" she whispered to Foxglove.

"I hear it," said Foxglove. "What is it?"

Laurel listened more carefully. The sound was the chanting of many troll voices. It seemed to be coming from the dark bog that surrounded the village.

"The troll king must be close," said Laurel.

"What are we going to do?" Foxglove asked with a gulp.

"I don't know. But the feast begins soon, and—"

A noise came from the other cage and Laurel turned to look. Chitters was jumping up and down.

"Listen!" the chipmunk called.

"We are," Laurel said. "The troll king is coming."

"No. Not that. Something else!" cried Chitters. "Listen!"

Then they heard it. A faint voice from under their cage. Faint and familiar. A pair of bright eyes shone in the firelight.

"Mistletoe!" Laurel exclaimed. "Oh, Mistletoe. Get out of here before the trolls see you."

"Shhh!" warned the mouse. "I've got something for you."

Mistletoe bent down and picked up a leather cord with her teeth. The mouse tried to jump up to the floor of the cage. But the object at the end of the cord was too heavy for her to lift.

"Wait," whispered Laurel. "I can help."

Laurel reached into her cloak and pulled out her flute. She stuck one end of the instrument through the bars. The flute dipped a bit as Mistletoe climbed aboard.

Slowly and carefully, Laurel pulled the flute into the cage. Mistletoe rode along. The cord was between her teeth. And at the end of that cord was...

"A key!" whispered Laurel.

"Is that the key to these cages?" asked Foxglove.

"I hope so," replied Mistletoe. She dropped the key into Foxglove's hands.

"But how did you get it?" asked Foxglove.

"And how did you get here?" added Laurel.

They listened while Mistletoe explained that she had followed Laurel and Chitters after they were captured. She'd been in the troll village ever since, watching and waiting. And she'd noticed that one troll had a key hanging from his belt.

"That's Fang," said Foxglove.

"I saw him go into a hut," the mouse went on. "I followed him and found that he'd fallen asleep. So I chewed through the cord and took the key."

"Oh, Mistletoe," said Laurel softly. "That was very brave."

"It sure was," Foxglove agreed. "But we'd better get out of here now. Come on!"

The pixie reached through the bars of the cage. He stuck the key in the lock and started to turn it. Just then two trolls came by. Foxglove quickly snatched back the key.

"This isn't good," whispered Foxglove. "Even if we open the cage, we won't be able to get past the trolls. And we have to get Chitters too."

"Don't forget me!" cried the chipmunk. "Absolutely not!"

"We'd never leave you here," Laurel promised. "Even if it means we can't go."

By now the chanting had gotten much louder. Finally a line of marching trolls thundered into the village. At the end of the parade came the biggest, ugliest troll they'd seen yet.

The other trolls bowed as the huge troll marched by.

"The king!" gasped Laurel. "Look at him!"

In spite of the mud and dirt covering him, the king sparkled in the firelight. On his head sat a crown of bright gold. A jeweled belt circled his waist. And gemstones glittered from cuffs on his wrists.

The king turned and stared around the camp. Eyeing the pile of riches, he threw his head back and roared with laughter.

"Juicy prizes, my people!" the king shouted. "Wonderful treasures for your king. His majesty is satisfied."

Fang approached the king, bowing low. "A special gift, most high," said the troll. He pointed toward the cages holding Laurel and her friends.

"Ah!" bellowed the king. He clapped Fang on the back and headed over to the cages. Quickly Mistletoe hid in Foxglove's pocket.

"A pixie!" shouted the king as he peered into the cage. "And a woodfairy! What an honor—for you, that is." He gave an evil chuckle.

Then the king turned to the small cage. "And a tender treat for the end of the feast," he said as he looked at Chitters. "Fang, your king is pleased."

With that, the king moved to his throne and sat down. He clapped his hands twice. A young troll hurried over with a basket of food. Another brought a mug of swamp water.

As the king began to eat, the other trolls sat down. Soon all were stuffing themselves. They guzzled mug after mug of swamp water to wash down the rotten food.

From their cages, Laurel and her friends watched the horrible scene. The air became darker and smokier. The terrible smells of dirty trolls and moldy food drifted through the air. And every moment, the prisoners grew more afraid of what was to come.

Suddenly one large troll stumbled to his feet, spilling swamp water on those sitting nearby.

"A song!" he exclaimed, raising his half-empty mug into the air. "A song to celebrate our king! And his great treasure!" He began singing in an off-key croak. Before long the other trolls joined in.

Laurel was horrified. She clapped her hands over her ears to keep out the awful sound.

"Even *I* know that's not a song," muttered Foxglove.

The king seemed pleased at first. He tapped one clawed foot and beat a hand against his knee. But then his sharp ears caught a sound he didn't like. He leaned forward and listened closely.

Without warning, the king jumped up from his throne into the crowd of singing trolls. He grabbed a small troll and dragged him away from the others.

"You were singing in tune!" the king yelled, shaking the little troll. "How dare you! His majesty's ears hurt! His stomach aches! Do you want to make your king crazy?"

The king dropped the little troll in the mud. Trembling, the little troll crept off in shame. After a moment, the others started up their loud, ugly song again. And the king went back to his happy clapping and tapping.

"That's it!" cried Foxglove.

"What do you mean?" asked Laurel.

"The trolls can't stand music that's in tune. It drives them crazy. You can play something beautiful. If it really does hurt their ears, maybe we can make a break for it."

"You've never heard me play the flute," said Laurel doubtfully.

"So?"

"I've never played beautifully in my life. At least not for more than a few seconds at a time," said Laurel.

"Well, you have to try," replied Foxglove. "It's our only chance."

Laurel's hands shook as she picked up her flute. She wondered whether Foxglove's plan would work. What if

64

beautiful music didn't really drive trolls crazy? What if it just made them angry—and even meaner?

Laurel raised the flute to her lips. She began to play the tune she'd been practicing for the Celebration. I hope I can remember all the notes, she thought.

At first Laurel's flute just squeaked faintly. The trolls never noticed it over the sound of their own ugly singing. But then Laurel stopped thinking about finding the right notes. Or about playing for the Celebration. She thought only of her friends and how to save them.

Laurel's music filled the air. The notes grew stronger and more lovely. One by one, the trolls fell silent. They turned to stare at the cage and at Laurel.

The king let out a wild howl. Then the other trolls began to howl too. For a moment, Laurel was sure they were going to attack her. She closed her eyes and went on playing.

Then she heard Foxglove. "Keep playing! It's working!"

Laurel took a quick peek. Trolls were holding their ears and rolling all over the muddy ground.

She continued to play.

Foxglove put the key in the lock, turned it, and opened the cage door. He and Mistletoe jumped out of the cage and ran toward Chitters. Laurel stopped playing, grabbed her bag, and jumped out too.

But as soon as Laurel's flute fell silent, the trolls started scrambling to their feet.

"Don't stop yet!" shouted Foxglove.

So Laurel stood still and played her tune. How she longed to run—and run fast. But she forced herself to stay. And suddenly she realized—

Her song was about freedom! Now that she knew that,

she could play it perfectly.

While Laurel played, Foxglove opened the chipmunk's cage. Then the pixie dashed around the trolls and up to the king's treasure pile. He grabbed the Crystal and raced back toward Laurel.

"You can stop now!" called Foxglove. "Let's go!"

Laurel took a breath. "Go ahead!" she cried. "I'll catch up!"

She lifted the flute to her lips again and went on with her tune. If I stop now, she thought, they'll catch us. We'll never get away. And the trolls will have the Crystal forever.

Foxglove knew what Laurel was thinking. But still he waited. Finally he said, "Okay. I'll take the Crystal. Follow us as quickly as you can."

Foxglove and the two animals ran from the firelit space. In an instant, they were swallowed up by the darkness.

Laurel faced the trolls. As she played, she slowly backed across the open area. Once she stumbled. But she never stopped playing.

At the edge of the bog, Laurel's feet sank into the muddy ground. For another long moment, she played, watching the trolls roll about in the firelight. Then she whirled around and took off to catch up with her friends.

Behind her, trolls began to shout. The king's voice could be heard over all the rest.

"Get her!" he roared. "Get that miserable woodfairy!"

CHAPTER TEN

Flight to Freedom

aurel moved as fast as her wings could carry her. The dark bog was lit by only a sliver of moon. In the pale light, the short, twisted trees cast terrifying shadows.

Laurel made her escape along the same trail the trolls had taken to their village. By now the muddy swamp had swallowed up the trolls' footprints. But broken branches and smashed bushes marked the way they had come.

As the frightened fairy flew into the night, she tried to catch sight of her friends. It was hopeless! She couldn't see or hear them.

Yet she *could* hear the roar of angry trolls and the snapping of branches. The horrible creatures were already after her!

Laurel realized that she could fly no farther. She stopped to rest her tired wings.

"Foxglove!" she called. "Foxglove, where are you?"

There was no answer. For the first time that day, Laurel felt like giving up. I can't get out of the bog by myself, she thought. I just can't.

Then she heard a familiar voice.

"Laurel," Foxglove called softly. "We're right ahead of you. Keep coming."

Laurel hurried down the trail toward the sound of

Foxglove's voice. The smelly, sticky mud sucked at her shoes. Heavy vines struck her head and shoulders. But she kept going.

Laurel flew over a huge tree that had fallen across the trail. There was Foxglove, waiting in the moonlight. The Crystal was still under his arm. And Chitters and Mistletoe were at his feet.

"Oh, Foxglove," Laurel cried. "I'm so glad to see you."

"Not nearly as glad as we are to see you," said Foxglove. "I didn't like going ahead without you."

He gave a terrified glance in the direction of the troll village. "Now I think we'd better get moving!"

Laurel knew that Foxglove was right. It sounded like the trolls were getting closer.

"They can move faster than we can in this mud," she said. "We have to get off the path."

"Off the path?" questioned Foxglove. "If we do that, we'll be lost here forever."

"And if we don't," replied Laurel, "they'll catch us. We'll be prisoners forever."

Laurel waited a moment for that to sink in. Then she added, "Besides, I know you can find the way."

Foxglove shook his head. "I hope you're right," he said quietly.

Laurel quickly handed him her bag. "Here," she said. "Put the Crystal in this. It'll be easier to carry that way."

Foxglove did as Laurel suggested. Then he turned and stepped off the trail into the muddy bog. Laurel and the two animals followed.

Laurel saw that Foxglove stayed off the swampy ground as much as possible. He jumped lightly from stump to stump or ran along fallen trees. She followed as best she could by fluttering and jumping along behind.

The animals made good time too. Mistletoe leapt from one dry spot to the next. Meanwhile, Chitters had taken to the trees.

Laurel was beginning to think that they might outrun the trolls. If they could just keep going—

Then they reached a huge patch of mud. There wasn't a rotted log or tuft of grass to be seen. And there was no way to tell how deep the mud might be.

Chitters voiced all their thoughts. "Now what?" he asked. "What can we do? Where can we go?"

Foxglove turned to Laurel. "Do you think you can fly over this?" he asked.

"I'll try," she answered bravely. "But what about the rest of you?"

"I have an idea," he said. The pixie snapped two leafy branches from a nearby bush.

"What are you going to do?" asked Laurel.

"Just watch!" said Foxglove. He reached into a pocket and pulled out two long strips of cloth. "This is all that's left of my cloak," he said with a grin.

The pixie put one foot on top of each branch. Quickly he tied the branches to his feet.

In spite of her fear, Laurel laughed. "You've made duck feet!" she exclaimed.

"That's right," said the pixie. "This mud looks thick enough to hold me up."

He placed the two animals on his shoulder. "Hold on tight," he ordered. Grabbing a long stick, he edged out onto the mud.

Foxglove's plan worked. The branches held him up. And the stick helped him keep his balance. Slowly but steadily, he plodded across the mud patch.

Laurel spread her wings and flew after her friends. She and Foxglove reached the other side at the same time.

Foxglove untied the branches from his feet. Then the four friends rested for a minute.

But as tired as they were, they had to keep moving. The trolls were still close behind them.

"Let's hurry," said Laurel. "I think we're almost to the river."

As she spoke, a passing cloud blotted out the moon. The little bit of light that had guided them vanished.

"We can't do it!" exclaimed Foxglove. "It's too dangerous to walk through here in the dark."

"We have to," said Laurel. "The trolls are getting closer!"

She blindly stepped forward, but her foot sank deep into the mud. "You're right," she said with a sob. "We can't go on. Not without a light."

Then it hit her. The Crystal! The inside of the Crystal sparkled with its own light!

But the Crystal was never opened—except during the Celebration. And even then, it was never opened by a fairy as young as Laurel.

If we don't get out of here, she thought, there will be no Crystal. And no Celebration.

"Foxglove!" Laurel called into the darkness. "The Crystal!"

His voice came from beside her. "Don't worry, I still have it," he said.

"Open it!" said Laurel.

"What?"

"I said, open it!" she cried.

A rainbow of color lit the dark bog. Foxglove held the brilliant stone in front of him. He stared in wonder at the hundreds of tiny glittering crystals inside.

"It's beautiful," breathed Foxglove. "The most beautiful thing I've ever seen."

"Can you carry it that way?" asked Laurel.

"Yes," the pixie answered. "But you'd better take this." He handed Laurel the Chronicles, which had rested inside the Crystal.

Laurel clasped the book firmly against her side. "Let's hurry," she said.

Foxglove set out across the swampy ground, holding the Crystal tightly in his arms. With its light, they easily spotted the dry places. And the sound of rushing water soon led them to the river.

"This way," said Foxglove as he headed to the right. "The tree bridge can't be far."

His friends followed the pixie along the river's edge. Once Foxglove almost slipped on the muddy bank. But he never lost his hold on the Crystal.

"There it is!" cried Laurel. "There's the bridge!" She moved ahead of Foxglove. "Hurry!" she called.

With a racing heart, Laurel waited until her friends had all reached the fallen tree. "Chitters and Mistletoe, you two go first," she said.

The animals darted over the bridge, the Crystal lighting their way. Now it was Laurel and Foxglove's turn.

Laurel stared at the river uneasily. The water had risen since earlier in the day. Now the river tugged steadily at the fallen tree, causing it to shift and roll slightly. Would the bridge hold up under their weight?

Laurel was too tired to fly anymore. She'd have to cross on foot. But neither she nor Foxglove could do that while trying to balance the open Crystal. And without its light, they wouldn't be able to see their way. What were they to do?

At that moment, the clouds parted. Pale moonlight filled the swamp once more.

Foxglove sighed. "Just in time. Give the Chronicles back to me, Laurel."

Laurel handed him the book. He shut it inside the Crystal and tucked the whole thing back into Laurel's bag. Then the pixie jumped lightly onto the fallen tree.

The bridge creaked under his feet. But Foxglove said bravely, "Come on, Laurel. We can do it."

"Not both of us at once," said Laurel. "I don't think it will hold us. You go first. Get the Crystal across the river."

Foxglove gave her a worried look. At last he nodded. "All right. I'll cross and then open the Crystal again to give you more light."

He put Laurel's bag over his shoulder. Bending low, he carefully crossed the shaky bridge. When he was safely on the other side, he opened the Crystal.

Laurel forced herself to stay calm and not think about the trolls close behind. Fluttering her wings for balance, she began to tiptoe across the fallen tree. The bridge rocked with every step.

After what seemed like forever, Laurel reached the other side. Foxglove helped her off the bridge. Then he closed the Crystal and put it in the bag. "Come on!" he said. "The trolls will be here any minute!"

But Laurel grabbed his arm. "Wait!"

"What?"

"The bridge," said Laurel. "We have to get rid of it! Otherwise, the trolls will follow us all the way to the Dappled Woods."

"Get rid of the bridge?" questioned Foxglove. "How? That tree is huge."

"The river has already started to move it," said Laurel. "We just need to finish the job somehow."

"I've got an idea!" Mistletoe exclaimed.

The mouse ran to the ropes that held the tree in place. "I'll chew through the ropes," she said. "And the bridge will fall into the water."

"Won't work," said Chitters. "Not at all! They're too thick!"

"It *has* to work, Chitters," answered Mistletoe.

The chipmunk nodded. "Let's try. Certainly!" He leapt beside Mistletoe and began chewing.

"We can help," said Laurel. "Come on, Foxglove. Grab a rock, and let's try to cut through these ropes."

Soon all four were hard at work. The ropes fell away until there was just one left. The only way to reach it was to step onto the tree.

Suddenly several huge trolls burst through the underbrush on the other side of the river. Close behind them were others. Even over the noise of the rushing water, Laurel could hear their shouts.

Foxglove dropped his rock. "Let's go!" he shouted.

"There's still one more rope," Laurel said. She jumped

onto the tree and began sawing at the rope.

"Laurel, watch out!" Foxglove called.

Laurel glanced up to see a huge troll step boldly out onto the bridge. She saw a glint of gold in the moonlight. It was the troll king!

Laurel lowered her head and sawed wildly.

"Laurel!" Foxglove screamed. "Leave it! Now!"

Laurel looked up again. The troll was nearly upon her! His eyes were glittering with hatred. He let out a horrible laugh and reached for her with his huge, clawed hand.

The Return of the Crystal

nap!

The last rope broke. At once the tree bridge fell toward the water. Instead of grabbing Laurel, the troll king threw himself flat against the tree trunk. Quickly he wrapped his arms and legs around it.

In just moments, the water would carry the tree—and its passengers—away from the riverbank. As tired as she was, Laurel's only hope was to fly. She slowly rose into the air.

At the same time, the tree began moving. Laurel found herself high above the rushing water.

But she couldn't fly another inch. Laurel began to sink.

A hand firmly gripped her wrist. Foxglove had reached far out over the water to grab Laurel. Now he tugged her toward him. In a few seconds, she felt solid earth beneath her feet.

Laurel breathlessly fell to the ground near Foxglove. She watched as the tree drifted away with the troll king aboard.

But ropes still held the tree in place on the other bank. So now it swung around and rolled toward that side of the river.

Before the tree could hit the bank, the king rose to his feet and jumped. He slipped wildly on the muddy slope. Finally he got his footing. He climbed to safety just as the tree broke loose.

The king watched in angry silence as the bridge floated out of sight downstream. Then he turned to Laurel and her companions. He raged at them, screaming a stream of curses.

At last he shook his fist, turned away, and headed back to his village. The other trolls followed, shouting their own curses.

"Well, I guess they'll be sticking to their bog from now on," said Foxglove.

"For a while," replied Laurel. "But what if another tree falls across the river?"

"There's always that chance," said Foxglove. "So we have to be on guard."

"Even in the Dappled Woods," said Laurel sadly.

Laurel, Foxglove, and the animals were safe once more. But they were too worn out to celebrate. The four simply turned and walked off along the trail.

They had no trouble finding their way through the night forest. It wasn't as dark on this side of the river. Stars sparkled overhead, and the moonlight seemed brighter.

It was still night when they reached New Warren and crossed into the Dappled Woods. And dawn had yet to come when they stood on the hill above Thunder Falls.

Laurel looked longingly at the starlit waterfall. How good it would feel to wash off the stink of troll! Then she glanced at her treehouse. And how nice it would be to sink into her clean bed!

But she had something else to do first.

"We'd better get the Crystal back right away," she said softly to Foxglove.

The pixie nodded. He and the animals joined Laurel as she made her way to the Ancient Clearing.

All was quiet in the clearing. Moonlight trickled through the branches and circled the tree stump.

Foxglove turned to Laurel. He slipped her bag off his shoulder and carefully removed the Crystal.

"Here it is," he said, holding the Crystal out to Laurel.

Laurel shook her head. "No," she said softly. "You saved it. You should be the one to put it back where it belongs."

"I certainly didn't save it by myself," Foxglove objected. "In fact, I remember you saving me." Then he smiled. "But I accept the honor."

He carefully placed the Crystal inside the stump.

Laurel sighed a deep, contented sigh. "I'm going to stay and watch until everyone else wakes up," she said. "I'm afraid that the trolls will find some way to get the Crystal back."

"I'll stay with you," said Foxglove. "Until morning."

"And we'll be nearby," said Mistletoe. She hurried off to a hole at the edge of the clearing.

"Not far away," chattered Chitters. "Just call." He followed Mistletoe.

Laurel and Foxglove settled down on the soft grass. "Thank you," whispered Laurel. "For everything you did." In a matter of seconds, the woodfairy was fast asleep.

For a time, Foxglove simply sat and kept watch. When a cool breeze began to stir, he looked over at Laurel. Then he stood and walked to a bench at the edge of the clearing. He picked up a soft blanket and covered his friend.

"I'm sure the fairy who made this won't mind," whispered Foxglove. "Not after what you've done."

He moved back to the bench and lay down. He only meant to close his eyes for a moment. But he was soon sound asleep too.

Voices awakened Laurel. At least one voice was loud and angry. The trolls! she thought. The trolls are after us!

Then she realized that the loud, angry voice belonged to Mistress Gooseberry. And the other voice was Foxglove's.

"Thief!" shouted Mistress Gooseberry. "Pixie thief!"

"No!" cried Foxglove. "No, you don't understand!" He sounded frightened.

Laurel struggled to sit up. A soft, warm blanket covered her head and shoulders. She threw it off and jumped to her feet.

Foxglove was standing at the edge of the clearing. In front of him, her back to Laurel, was Mistress Gooseberry. She had a stick in one hand and was waving it wildly.

Other fairies had heard the noise. They stood behind Mistress Gooseberry and stared coldly at Foxglove. Even Mistress Marigold was frowning.

No one had seen Laurel. And no one had seemed to notice that the Crystal had been returned.

"How dare you come back here!" Mistress Gooseberry shouted again. "Trying to steal more from us, are you?"

Laurel angrily called out, "He's not a thief!"

At the sound of her voice, all the fairies turned around. Ivy darted forward with a glad cry. "Laurel! You're back!"

But Mistress Gooseberry broke in. "Where have you been?" she said.

"I've been with Foxglove," answered Laurel.

"Foxglove?" murmured the other fairies.

"Who?" said Mistress Gooseberry.

"Foxglove," repeated Laurel. "My friend." She walked across the clearing to stand beside the pixie.

Mistress Gooseberry turned red with anger. "I might have

guessed you had something to do with this!" she snapped. "What are you doing making friends with a pixie thief?"

"I told you, he's not a thief," said Laurel. "And if you don't believe me, just look."

She pointed to the stump. Mistress Marigold shot a questioning glance at Laurel, then hurried over to the stump. She threw open the door and stepped back to reveal the Crystal.

Mistress Gooseberry's jaw dropped. The rest of the wood-fairies gasped.

Mistress Gooseberry turned to Laurel and Foxglove. "I don't know how the Crystal got here," she said. "But I still think that pixie took it!"

"Let me explain," begged Laurel. "Please, just listen."

Mistress Marigold laid a hand on Mistress Gooseberry's sleeve. "Let's hear what Laurel has to say," she said gently. "She seems to know more about this than any of us."

Laurel gave Mistress Marigold a thankful look. Then she stared out at the crowd. "Foxglove is the one who brought the Crystal back to us. He's a hero!"

She went on. "But Mistress Gooseberry is right about one thing. I did have something to do with all this. I gave Foxglove permission to stay here in the Dappled Woods for a time."

Cries of shock ran through the crowd.

"While he was here, Foxglove saw a troll steal the Crystal," she continued. "He set out to save it—without even thinking about his own safety."

"A troll!" snapped Mistress Gooseberry. "There's no such thing!"

"Oh, yes there is," said Laurel. "I've seen one. Many of them, in fact. They're horrible!"

She went on to tell the whole story. She explained how

she first met the pixie. She described their scavenging trip into the Great Forest. And the second trip, when they had been captured by trolls. She also told how the music of her flute had helped them escape.

At the end of the story, the other fairies stared at her in silence. Laurel held her breath. Did they believe her? Did they understand that Foxglove was really a hero?

Mistress Marigold spoke for them all. "What an amazing story!" she said. "And what an amazing pair you are." She hugged Laurel. Then she turned to Foxglove.

"Thank you," she said warmly. "Thank you for saving the Crystal—and the Chronicles."

The pixie blushed and ducked his head.

Most of the fairies quickly forgot their natural shyness. They gathered around Foxglove and asked all kinds of questions. They wanted to know about pixies and where they lived. And they wanted to thank him for saving the Crystal from the trolls.

Finally Mistress Marigold raised her hand. The fairies grew quiet. "I think we should invite Foxglove to the Celebration tomorrow," she suggested.

A buzz went through the group. Many said, "Yes! Of course! Please stay!"

But others—like Mistress Gooseberry and Primrose—looked uncertain.

It would be a long time before some fairies were ready to accept a pixie. Laurel understood this. And she could see that Foxglove did too.

"Thanks," smiled Foxglove. "But I can't stay. I've been away from home for too long. It's time for me to say good-bye."

Laurel felt a lump form in her throat. "You're leaving right now?" she asked. "But you still haven't scavenged anything. You can't go home empty-handed."

Foxglove shrugged. But before he could reply, Mistress Marigold cleared her throat. "I really can't use this anymore," she said.

She took off a green scarf with a tiny hole in one end. Then she dropped it on the ground at the pixie's feet.

The other fairies whispered among themselves. One stepped forward with a cracked wooden button. Then Ivy dropped a broken necklace and a shell comb with a missing tooth. Others went off to return with used treasures of all kinds. Soon a pile of wonderful objects lay at Foxglove's feet.

"This will make me the greatest scavenger of all," laughed Foxglove. He smiled and gathered everything into a bag someone had placed on the pile.

"Wait just a minute, young pixie," said Mistress Gooseberry. Foxglove gave her a nervous glance.

"I think you forgot this," she said. She reached into a bag at her waist and took out a wooden whistle. "Here," she said with a sniff.

Foxglove grinned as he accepted it. He bowed to her and then to them all. "It has been a real pleasure, ladies," he said.

He turned to Laurel and smiled. "If you ever feel like wandering around the Great Forest again, just sing out. Especially if you're in the mood for some scavenging."

"I will," Laurel whispered.

Foxglove took a deep breath. He gave a last glance around the clearing and raised his hand in farewell.

As he set off, several fairies called out. They said something they'd never said to an outsider before. "Come back and visit us!" they cried.

"I will!" called Foxglove with a final wave. With that, he disappeared into the trees.

CHAPTER TWELVE

Laurel's Contribution

unlight shimmered through the curtains of Laurel's canopy bed. She sat up and stretched. She had rested most of the day before. But she still felt stiff and sore all over.

Laurel got up and threw on her robe. As she fixed breakfast, she thought of all that had happened in the past few days. Remembering the ugly, frightening trolls wasn't pleasant. But thinking about Foxglove and their new friendship made Laurel smile.

"I'm sure he'll be back," she said to herself.

She took her breakfast out on the porch. Chitters and Mistletoe were waiting for her.

"Good morning," called the animals.

"Good morning to you," answered Laurel. She scooped some nuts and berries from the bowl and offered them to her friends.

"We had quite an adventure, didn't we?" sighed Laurel. "I wrote in my journal for hours yesterday. All about the trolls. And escaping and bringing the Crystal back. I didn't want to forget a thing."

"I'll never forget!" said Chitters. "Never! Never! Never!"

Laurel laughed at the little chipmunk. Then her eyes fell upon the dress she'd worn into the Great Forest. It hung over the porch railing where she'd put it to dry.

"And I have my dress to remind me too," she said. "I'm afraid it's ruined. I washed the mud out in the waterfall. But it's torn and tattered."

"I know," said Mistletoe. "My fur isn't in the best shape either."

Then Laurel had an idea. "I could use this dress for scraps," she said softly. "And start making a quilt. Just like the pixies do."

That would make a fine offering for next year's Celebration, she thought. A very different one too.

Thinking about next year made Laurel jump to her feet. For today was this year's Celebration. It was almost time to start!

Laurel went back inside. She quickly changed into a clean dress and cloak. Then she smoothed her hair and put on a headband. "There! That will have to do," she said to herself. She grabbed her flute and rushed outside.

"Good-bye," she called to Mistletoe and Chitters.

"Good luck!" they called back.

Laurel headed straight for the Ancient Clearing. Halfway there she heard a lovely tinkling sound.

Laurel smiled. After hearing her story yesterday, Mistress Marigold had made a wonderful suggestion. The fairies could make wind chimes. That way, if another troll came into the Dappled Woods, the music of the chimes would drive the thief away.

So the woodfairies had done just that. Now their chimes of wood and shells hung all around the Ancient Clearing.

By the time Laurel reached the clearing, most of the other fairies were already waiting. The Crystal had been moved from the stump to a place of honor at the center of the clearing.

Laurel hurried over to group of young fairies. Spotting a space between Ivy and Primrose, she sat down.

"Thank goodness you're here," said Ivy. "I was afraid you'd gone on another adventure."

"No, I just lost track of time," admitted Laurel.

Primrose sniffed. She never lost track of time. And she was never late.

But Primrose didn't have a chance to say anything. The Celebration was about to start.

All the elders gathered in the center of the clearing. Then a very old fairy stepped forward. She was the Eldest—the keeper of fairy history.

Carefully the Eldest opened the Crystal. A rainbow of color flooded the clearing.

The Crystal had been beautiful when it lit the way through the dark bog. But Laurel thought it looked even more lovely now. She wished Foxglove could be here to see it.

"Well," she whispered to herself, "maybe next year."

The Eldest removed the Chronicles from the Crystal. She placed the old book on a polished wooden stand. Then she nodded to all the fairies and quietly spoke.

"Every year we turn back the pages of the Chronicles to some point in our past. We read about what happened then.

That's our way."

The Eldest gently opened the Chronicles and turned the pages. She found the spot she wanted and began reading in a firm voice.

Laurel listened as the Eldest told of a year long past. A year in which woodfairies had created wonderful music and art and dance. Just as they had always done. And just as they would always do.

For a moment, thoughts of the ugly troll village arose in Laurel's mind. But the gleaming Crystal erased the picture. She was beginning to understand how important the work of the woodfairies was. For in their art, they captured all that was good and beautiful about the forest.

The Eldest finished reading. A hush hung over the Ancient Clearing. Then she spoke again.

"The time has come to record this year's entry. In that way, many years from now, other woodfairies can read about what we did."

She picked up a pen. "This year, Mistress Marigold will write for us," she announced.

Mistress Marigold took the pen and looked out over the gathering.

"For as long as I can remember," she began, "we have started with the same words. Every year we write, 'We did many beautiful, creative things this year.'"

Most of the other woodfairies smiled and nodded at the familiar words.

"But this year, our entry will begin a bit differently," said Mistress Marigold.

The fairies stared at one another in amazement.

Mistress Marigold bent over the book. As she wrote, she

read her words aloud. "We did many beautiful, creative, *and exciting* things this year," she said. Then she looked up at the others.

"Now I'll add your words," she announced.

She started with the elders. In turn, each fairy told of one special thing that had happened in the past year. Mistress Marigold carefully recorded their words about what they'd seen, created, and done.

Finally it was time for Laurel to share.

"Laurel," said Mistress Marigold. "What would you like me to write?"

As Laurel stood, her mind raced. So much had happened. What did she most want to have remembered?

Suddenly she knew. "If you please, here is what I'd like written: This year I met a pixie. And we became friends."

Mistress Marigold nodded and smiled. Then she added Laurel's words to the Chronicles.

At last she was done recording. It was time for the young woodfairies to perform. So they danced their dances, read their poems, showed their paintings, and sang their songs. And how wonderful it all was! Every performance reminded Laurel of the beauty of the woods. She was especially proud as Ivy offered her dance of the violet.

Laurel had worried about her own contribution for so long. But now, when her turn came, she was totally calm. She walked to the center of the clearing.

Laurel took a deep breath. As she raised her flute, she noticed two small heads pop up from the bushes. Mistletoe and Chitters had come to hear her.

Laurel closed her eyes and played. It was a haunting, beautiful tune. So beautiful that it had driven the trolls half

crazy! Thanks to this tune, she and her friends had escaped to freedom. And now the music perfectly captured the beauty and freedom of the Dappled Woods.

For the second time, Laurel played her song without missing a single note.

More to Explore

Have fun exploring more about the creatures of folklore. And there are great projects for you to do too!

Magical Creatures of Folklore

People have long told tales about magical creatures such as fairies, pixies, and trolls. These beings may be beautiful or nightmarish. Funny or frightening. Helpful or harmful. In fact, sometimes they are all of these things at once.

At one time, many people believed these magical creatures actually existed. Now the stories about them are just that: entertaining folktales.

Folktales are usually told, not written down. So they pass from one person to the next and from one country to another. As they do, the tales change and sometimes blend together. That's why a dwarf and a troll, for instance, might seem a lot alike.

Here are a few magical characters from folklore.

Peris

The peri is a fairylike creature from Persian stories. (Persia is now Iran.) Peris can be found in cities of jewels in the mountains. Instead of eating, they live off sweet scents. Their bodies are made of fire and they are said to be marvelously beautiful.

Fairies

Stories about fairies are found in many countries. These beings are some of the most beautiful, playful, and undependable creatures in folklore. Fairies can bless or curse a baby. They bring happiness to some humans—and bewitch others.

Fairies are graceful folk who love music and dancing. In fact, trails in the dewy grass may be your only clue that fairies spent the night waltzing there. Perhaps it's because fairies are so hard to see that storytellers don't agree about their size. Some describe fairies as the size of an acorn, while others say they are as tall as humans.

Dwarves

Dwarves are found in many tales from Germany and Scandinavia. Like the little men who befriend Snow White, they are small creatures. And they are usually very old. In some ways, dwarves are like trolls—especially in their love of treasure.

Dwarves are known for creating wonderful, magical objects out of metal. Many dwarves live below ground (where they're close to the metals they need). Some myths say that if dwarves are struck by sunlight, they turn to stone.

Jinn

Jinn (or genii) come from Arabic cultures. There are good, beautiful jinn—as well as evil, ugly ones. Jinn have many powers. They can change form, turn invisible, and tell the future. If you see a whirlwind in the desert, you'll know an evil jinn is passing by.

Brownies

Brownies, dressed in their ragged cloaks of brown, roam the hills of Scotland. They are described as short, with curly hair and wrinkled faces. Brownies sometimes adopt families. They will do all kinds of favors and chores for the lucky household. In return, they merely hope for a nice meal left in a private corner. But if they think that gift is only given to make them stay around, they'll leave.

Pixies

Pixies, from England, can be just as helpful as brownies. But they also sometimes steal children, lead travelers astray, and take horses for wild rides. Pixies love to dance. Like brownies, pixies are small, but they prefer green clothing.

Elves

Elves inhabit many lands, including England. Forests and meadows are usually where you'll find these crea-  tures. However, evil elves prefer to live underground. Like many magical beings, elves love neatness. In fact, they reward people who are clean and orderly—and punish those who aren't.

Trolls

Trolls are part of Scandinavian myths. They have humped backs and long crooked noses. They build their homes of crystal and gold inside hills and mounds. Here they also store their huge chests of treasure. Trolls can offer both riches and strength to humans.

Keeping trouble away

As you can see, the old tales show that many magical creatures couldn't be trusted. Some people tried to get on their good side by leaving gifts such as clothing or food. Others thought it best to stay away from them altogether. The list that follows describes a few of the things people used to keep away unwelcome fairies, elves, and other mythical beings.

- drum beats
- clothing worn inside-out
- salt
- four-leaf clover
- running water
- horseshoe
- sock under the bed

These charms must have worked. After all, few people claim to see these magical creatures today. But they live on in the old and new stories we continue to tell about them.

Wind Chimes

The woodfairies' wind chimes filled the Dappled Woods with music. You can enjoy the lovely sound of wood chimes too. Just follow the directions below.

What you need

- Eight to ten sea shells*
- Awl or large nail
- Hammer
- Ruler
- Nylon fishing line (ten-pound test or thicker)
- Metal or plastic craft ring (¾" to 1" diameter)
- Wooden embroidery hoop (4" to 6" diameter)

*If you don't have shells, see the end of the activity for another wind chime idea.

What you do

1. Wash and dry the shells.

2. Ask an adult to help you punch a hanging hole in each shell. Be sure to work on a surface that can't be damaged, such as a workbench or ½"-thick board. Hold the point of the awl or large nail about 1" in from an outside edge of the shell. Use the hammer to push the awl or nail through the shell. (Some shells may break. You need to end up with at least five good shells.)

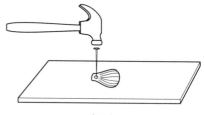

Step 2

96

3. Cut a 2' length of fishing line for each shell. Poke one end of the line through the hole in the shell and tie three or four knots. Leave at least an inch hanging at the knotted edge. You will trim this later. Set the strung shells aside.

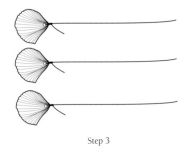

Step 3

4. Cut two 3' sections of fishing line. Fold them together at the middle, making an open loop. Slip the loop through the center of the craft ring. Then pull the loose ends through the loop as shown. You should have four loose ends hanging down. Trim the ends to make them all the same length.

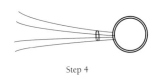

Step 4

5. Separate the two circles of the embroidery hoop. (You need only one circle for a set of wind chimes.) Tie the loose ends of the fishing line to the hoop, spacing them evenly around the edge. The hoop should hang about 6" to 8" below the craft ring. Again, tie each knot at least three or four times and leave an inch of fishing line hanging at the knotted edge.

Step 5

6. Hang the hoop by the craft ring so it is suspended in the air.

7. Begin tying the shells to the wooden hoop so they hang down about 8" to 10". Arrange them around the hoop so that it hangs fairly evenly. If you want, you can hang one shell from the craft ring by a 3' length of fishing line. Let it dangle down in the middle of the wind chimes.

8. Trim the fishing line as needed. Then hang your wind chimes inside, near a window.

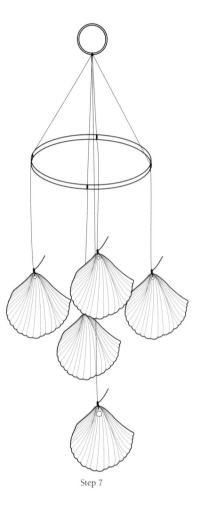

Step 7

Another wind chime idea

You don't have to have shells to make a wind chime. You can create shapes yourself from Play Clay. Use the recipe on the next page to make a batch of clay. Then follow the directions below.

1. Roll a ball of Play Clay out to ½" thickness.

2. With a sharp knife or cookie cutters, cut shapes. You can make shells, leaves, suns, stars, butterflies, trees,

flowers, or geometric shapes. Some shapes may break, so make a few extra. You want to have at least five good shapes for your wind chimes.

3. Use a nail or toothpick to make a hole about ½" from the top edge of each shape.

4. Carefully lift the shapes and place them on a flat surface to dry for at least 36 hours.

5. When the shapes are dry, you can decorate them with tempera paint. Be sure to paint both sides and then let the paint dry completely.

6. When your shapes are done, go to page 97. Follow steps 3 through 8 for the shell wind chimes, using your shapes in place of shells.

Play Clay

2 cups baking soda	1 cup cornstarch
1 1⁄4 cup water	

Combine the ingredients in a saucepan. Cook over medium heat, stirring constantly. When mixture becomes very thick and starts to pull away from the side of the pan, take the pan off the stove. Scrape the clay out of the pan and onto a dinner plate. Let it cool for at least an hour. Then knead the clay for a few minutes until it feels smooth. Store in an airtight container or plastic bag.

Woodland Cookbook

Try some of Laurel's favorite woodland recipes yourself. Then invite a friend to share them with you. You can serve your fairy treats at an outdoor picnic in the backyard. Or if you have a favorite tree or a treehouse, eat there. And if it's raining, get the treehouse feeling by serving your guest in the attic!

Be sure to get permission to use the stove and oven. Or ask an adult to help you.

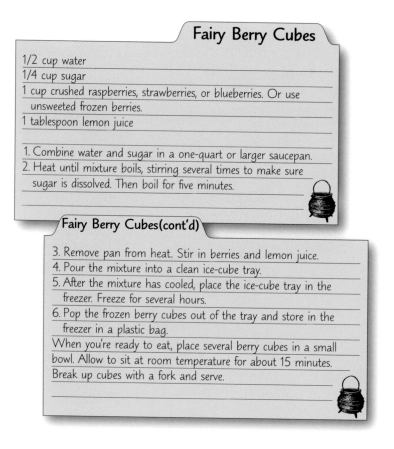

Fairy Berry Cubes

1/2 cup water

1/4 cup sugar

1 cup crushed raspberries, strawberries, or blueberries. Or use unsweeted frozen berries.

1 tablespoon lemon juice

1. Combine water and sugar in a one-quart or larger saucepan.
2. Heat until mixture boils, stirring several times to make sure sugar is dissolved. Then boil for five minutes.

Fairy Berry Cubes(cont'd)

3. Remove pan from heat. Stir in berries and lemon juice.
4. Pour the mixture into a clean ice-cube tray.
5. After the mixture has cooled, place the ice-cube tray in the freezer. Freeze for several hours.
6. Pop the frozen berry cubes out of the tray and store in the freezer in a plastic bag.

When you're ready to eat, place several berry cubes in a small bowl. Allow to sit at room temperature for about 15 minutes. Break up cubes with a fork and serve.

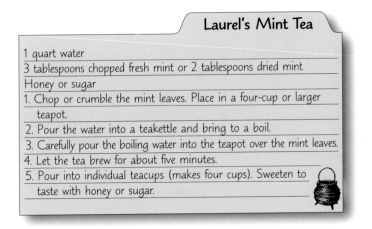

Laurel's Mint Tea

1 quart water

3 tablespoons chopped fresh mint or 2 tablespoons dried mint

Honey or sugar

1. Chop or crumble the mint leaves. Place in a four-cup or larger teapot.
2. Pour the water into a teakettle and bring to a boil.
3. Carefully pour the boiling water into the teapot over the mint leaves.
4. Let the tea brew for about five minutes.
5. Pour into individual teacups (makes four cups). Sweeten to taste with honey or sugar.

Ivy's Berry Nice Muffins

1 egg	1/4 cup sugar
3/4 cup milk	3 teaspoons baking powder
1/2 cup canola oil	1/2 teaspoon salt
2 cups whole wheat flour	1 cup blueberries or raspberries*

1. Heat oven to 400°. Place paper liners in cups of 12-count muffin pan. Or grease bottoms of cups.
2. Crack the egg and place in a large bowl. Beat with a fork.

Ivy's Berry Muffins(cont'd)

3. Add milk and oil, stirring until combined.
4. Add the rest of the ingredients, except for the berries. Stir just until combined.
5. Add berries and stir to mix.
6. Fill muffin cups about 3/4 full.
7. Bake until tops are browned, about 20 minutes.

*You can use unsweetened frozen berries. In this recipe, frozen berries don't need to be thawed first.

Stardust Story Sampler

Stardust Classics books feature other heroines to believe in. Come explore with Kat the Time Explorer and Alissa, Princess of Arcadia. Here are short selections from their books.

Selection from

KAT THE TIME EXPLORER

Kat sighed. There had to be some secret to the time machine. She and Jessie had gotten it put together. Now if they could just get it to work!

Slowly and carefully, Kat ran her hands over the surface of the machine. Inch by inch, her fingers pressed and prodded.

Kat was pressing on the left side of the machine when it happened. There was a tiny movement beneath her fingers.

"Jessie!" Kat cried. "I've found something!"

Jessie hurried over. While her aunt watched, Kat slid open a small, thin drawer.

"It's a secret compartment," said Kat. "You have to know just where to push!"

"What can it be for?" asked Jessie in excitement. "There's nothing in there."

"But look at the bottom of the drawer," said Kat. "See those hollow round spaces? I bet the medallions we found fit there!"

Quickly Jessie got the two medallions. Kat watched as her aunt popped them into place, chains and all.

Nothing happened. Then Jessie slid the drawer back into the machine. Nothing.

"Well, they fit," said Jessie. "But they don't seem to do

anything."

"I was hoping that they might be the power source for the machine," said Kat.

"It doesn't look like it," commented Jessie. "Still, let me check the notebook one more time. Perhaps I missed some clue about what they're for."

While Jessie paged through the notebook, Kat experimented with the medallions. "Maybe they have to go in another way," she whispered to herself.

First she put the silver one where the gold one had been. Then she flipped them over. Nothing happened.

Kat kept trying until there was only one possibility left. She placed the silver medallion on the right—with the front showing. She set the gold medallion on the left—with the back showing.

At once a strange humming sound filled the room!

"What's going on?" called Jessie. She jumped to her feet and started across the room. Grabbing the other end of the machine, she shouted, "Let go, Kat!"

But before Kat could move, a ray of sunlight shone through the small basement window. The light poured over the time machine and lit up the open drawer. The medallions began to glow. Swirling ribbons of mist rose up around Kat and Jessie.

In a matter of seconds, the basement lab faded from sight. Kat couldn't see or hear Jessie.

Suddenly a whistle screamed and the ground began to shake. Kat gazed about blindly, trying to make sense of it all. Where was she? And where was Jessie?

Just as she was about to shout Jessie's name, the mist parted. To her relief, Kat saw her aunt standing across from her.

But nothing else was familiar. The basement lab had vanished. Now they stood in the corner of a huge, domed building. People were rushing in every direction. And beside Kat and Jessie was a wall of gleaming black iron.

"It's a train!" cried Jessie. "An old-fashioned steam locomotive!"

As they watched, the train slowly inched forward. It came to a stop farther down the platform, hissing and spitting like a great dragon.

"What happened?" gasped Kat.

"It worked, Kat!" Jessie answered. "I don't know how, but it did!"

"We've really gone back into the past," whispered Kat.

Selection from

ALISSA, PRINCESS OF ARCADIA

"Good evening."

Princess Alissa jumped off the bench and spun around. Behind her stood an old man cloaked in a glittering robe.

"Who are you?" she asked. "And what are you doing here? Don't you know that these are the king's private gardens?"

"So they are," said the old man. "And where better to find a princess? For it's you I've come to talk to."

"To me?" said Alissa. "I don't mean to be rude, good sir. But why should I talk to you?"

"Perhaps for the same reason that you want to go on a quest," replied the stranger.

Alissa was startled. How did he know she'd been thinking about a quest?

She stared at the old man in wonder. In the moonlight she could see the long white beard that flowed almost to his waist. And she noticed how his cloak puffed and billowed, though there was no wind.

He continued. "Yes, Alissa, I know a good many things about you. For instance, I know you worry about your new responsibilities. And I think..."

Here he leaned closer and peered nearsightedly. "Just as I thought. You are searching for something."

"But how do you know all this about me?" Alissa asked. "I've never seen you before."

The old man closed his eyes for a moment. "Perhaps you have never seen me. But that doesn't mean I've never seen you."

He opened his eyes. "We will meet again, princess," he said.

"When? And how?" cried Alissa. Suddenly she realized that she wanted to see—had to see—this strange old man again. "And who are you? Where will I find you?"

"Ah," murmured the old man as he combed his fingers through his beard. "All good questions, Alissa. And perhaps a search for the answers should be your first quest."

"My first quest!" exclaimed Alissa. "Am I really to have a quest?"

"We shall see," said the old man. "We shall see. It all depends on you. But you'll need some help. So let this be your guide."

The old man drew himself up. He looked taller and younger—and much more powerful. In ringing tones, he said:

Unwind this riddle to its end
If you will seek this strange old man:
Find me where today becomes tomorrow,
Yet yesterdays still linger;
Where neither ground nor air is master.
In a shelter cloaked in danger.

As soon as he finished speaking, the old man turned to go. Alissa jumped up to follow. She cried out, "Wait! Please wait! What's that supposed to mean?"

But as she started forward, Alissa slipped on the wet ground. By the time she righted herself, all she could see was a swirl of mist. The old man had disappeared into the dark shadows.

"How could he have moved so quickly?" she asked. "Who is he? And what exactly does his riddle mean?" But she received no answers from the empty garden.

STARDUST CLASSICS titles are written under pseudonyms. Authors work closely with Margaret Hall, executive editor of Just Pretend.

Ms. Hall has devoted her professional career to working with and for children. She has a B.S. and an M.S. in education from the State University of New York at Geneseo. For many years, she taught as a classroom and remedial reading teacher for students from preschool through upper elementary. Ms. Hall has also served as an editor with an educational publisher and as a consultant for the Iowa State Department of Education. She has a long history as a freelance writer for the school market, authoring several children's books as well as numerous teacher resources.

JOEL SPECTOR, illustrator of *Laurel the Woodfairy,* was born in Cuba and moved to Queens, New York, when he was 12 years old. He graduated from the Fashion Institute of Technology in New York City and began his art career as a fashion illustrator.

Mr. Spector has illustrated many books and other materials. He provided illustrations for a Japanese series based on the Anne of Green Gables books. The series was intended for use in teaching English in Japan—where Anne is an extremely popular character.

Joel Spector lives in Connecticut with his wife and their four children. His eldest son, Max, was the model for Laurel's friend Foxglove.

PATRICK FARICY, the cover illustrator, was born and raised in Minnesota. He began his art education there, studying communication design, illustration, and fine art at the School of Associated Arts in St. Paul. He completed his studies at the Art Center College of Design in Pasadena, California.

Since graduating in 1991, Mr. Faricy has been living in California and working as a freelance illustrator. His clients include Coca-Cola, Kellogg's, Busch Gardens, and Warner Brothers.

When he's not painting, Patrick Faricy spends his time writing and playing music, going to the movies, and talking with friends. And he is always on the lookout for something new and different to add to his frog collection!

This Book Is Just the Beginning...

Order the new Just Pretend catalog to discover an entire fantasy world beyond the Stardust Classic stories. The Stardust collection includes beautiful dolls with gorgeous clothing, fairytale furniture, and accessories galore. You can set the stage for any adventure imaginable starring your favorite Stardust Classics characters.

Stardust
C L A S S I C S™

If the postcard is missing, you can still get a Just Pretend catalog, featuring the Stardust Classics books and dolls. Send your name and address to:

Just Pretend, Inc.
Stardust Classics
104 Challenger Drive
Portland, TN 37148-1729

Or call our toll-free number:

1-800-286-7166

You can also request a catalog online. Visit us at our Website!

www.justpretend.com

Ask for Stardust Classics at your library or bookstore.

NO POSTAGE
NECESSARY
IF MAILED
IN THE
UNITED STATES

BUSINESS REPLY MAIL
FIRST-CLASS MAIL   PERMIT NO. 587   PORTLAND TN

POSTAGE WILL BE PAID BY ADDRESSEE

Just Pretend, Inc.
104 Challenger Drive
Portland,TN 37148-9994